"Get your hands off me, you lecher!" she exclaimed.

He held her chin and pressed his lips firmly on hers. The harder she tried to escape, the more he persisted.

The arrogance of it! Yet she was not entirely immune. There was some secret pleasure in his ardent insistance. She had never been kissed in this fashion before. It was strangely exciting. A tumultuous flutter in her breast warned of the danger in this game.

Her push sent Rotham reeling back.

"You have finally succeeded in achieving perfection in one category, Rotham. What a perfectly rude, common, vulgar, repulsive creature you are."

"And you, madam, are a perfect shrew!"

UNICORN ONE
USED BOOKS
8028 W. GRAND RIVER
BRIGHTON, MI 48114
810-227-9894

By Joan Smith
Published by Fawcett Books:

THE SAVAGE LORD GRIFFIN
GATHER YE ROSEBUDS
AUTUMN LOVES: An Anthology
THE GREAT CHRISTMAS BALL
NO PLACE FOR A LADY
NEVER LET ME GO
REGENCY MASQUERADE
THE KISSING BOUGH
A REGENCY CHRISTMAS: An Anthology
DAMSEL IN DISTRESS
A KISS IN THE DARK
THE VIRGIN AND THE UNICORN

THE VIRGIN
AND
THE UNICORN

Joan Smith

FAWCETT CREST • NEW YORK

Sale of this book without a front cover may be unauthorized. If this book is coverless, it may have been reported to the publisher as "unsold or destroyed" and neither the author nor the publisher may have received payment for it.

A Fawcett Crest Book
Published by Ballantine Books
Copyright © 1995 by Joan Smith

All rights reserved under International and Pan-American Copyright Conventions. Published in the United States by Ballantine Books, a division of Random House, Inc., New York, and simultaneously in Canada by Random House of Canada Limited, Toronto.

Library of Congress Catalog Card Number: 95-90346

ISBN 0-449-22380-9

Manufactured in the United States of America

First Edition: September 1995

10 9 8 7 6 5 4 3 2 1

Chapter One

Twilight was falling when they came to take Rotham's body away. Dinner had been over for some time, but the sun lingers long in June. Miranda watched them from the doorway of the Tapestry Room, which gave a view of the front staircase. Four footmen carried the litter holding the body, with the gray blanket pulled over that handsome face she had grown to love. Impossible to think those eyes would never open again; those lips would never smile, or curse, or kiss. The covered body was carried gently upstairs, watched by Rotham's papa, Lord Hersham. The old man's feet moved unsteadily, and his head was bent in sorrow. It is hard work, burying a son.

Miranda could not believe Rotham was dead. It was like believing the sun had fallen from the sky, or the tide was not coming in. A numbness seized her. She was not even able to grieve yet. That would come later. She would have to learn to live in a world without him.

How could she do it? She would never waltz again without remembering her waltz with him, here in the ballroom at Ashmead just a few short nights ago.

He would be her invisible escort on future trips

to the nearby village of Rye, where they had gone last night to break into a house. Every time she mentioned Trudie's name she would see his lowering brow. As to ever kissing a gentleman again . . . What mere mortal could ever create the thrill that trembled up her spine and lifted the hairs on her arms, that sent her heart racing when Rotham kissed her?

She had never known Ashmead without Lord Rotham; he had been there before she was born. In every society there is one character who dominates, and in the coastal society of east Kent, it was Lord Rotham, the elder son and heir of the Marquess of Hersham. It was he who brought life to the place when he came down from London with his smart friends. He had balls and hunts, curricle races, and romances past counting with all the local belles. His name was always accompanied by a whiff of scandal. His women, his gambling, his fast lifestyle. Yet as the premier *parti* of the parish, and an exceedingly handsome one besides, his misdemeanors tended to enhance his reputation rather than tarnish it.

It was hoped at one time that he would offer for Miranda's older sister, Trudie, but in the end it had turned out to be only one of his flirtations. Of course, it had been aiming pretty high to hope the heir to Ashmead would offer for Miss Vale. Trudie was the beauty of the Vale family, however, and much is expected of beauty. She had satisfied expectations by marrying a baron, Lord Parnham, commonly known in Society as Lord Parsnip as a compliment to his long and pointy nose.

Less was expected of Miranda. She lived in the shade of the blond Incomparable. Her raven hair and dark eyes were her chief claims to beauty. Trudie told her that when she learned to "manage" her eyes and curb her wayward tongue, she would do very well in Society. She knew without having been told that her sister Sukey's having come down with the measles was only an excuse to send her to Ashmead for a few weeks. The reason was to foster a romance between her and Lord Pavel, Hersham's younger son. It might even have happened, had Lord Rotham not been there, although Miranda thought it extremely unlikely.

It was strange that Rotham was at home, for all the world knew he had been sent to the great Congress in Vienna as an assistant to Lord Wellington. But the Congress had broken down when Bonaparte escaped from Elba, and in early June Wellington had sent Rotham to England to handle some government business. He had stopped at Ashmead en route and seemed, strangely, in no hurry to continue on his way.

Miranda remembered the day he had returned. She had just arrived at Ashmead that morning. The afternoon had been spent sitting in this same Tapestry Room repairing a thirteenth-century Flemish tapestry. She was clever with a needle, but it took all her skill, for the old fabric on which she was working had been in tatters. Lady Hersham, a formidable dame of fifty-odd years, was with her, working at her high-warp loom. She was weaving a picture of Ashmead, with Lord Hersham and herself mounted on a pair of white horses riding in the park. She worked from a cartoon she had copied from a wedding portrait done by Gainsborough three decades before.

It was strange that in a mansion where nearly

every nook and cranny was hung with at least one tapestry, there were none hanging in the Tapestry Room. This was a work area given over to Lady Hersham's hobby, one might almost say her life. It was here, surrounded by baskets of silk and woolen threads, by shuttles and bobbins, that she worked at the loom, transposing pictures designed by some of the foremost artists of the day into wall hangings.

As darkness fell that evening of Rotham's death, Miranda could see a wavy image of the Ashmead tapestry mirrored in the darkened window, not quite clear, but insubstantial, as in a dream. She rose and wandered to the window, gazing at the reflection.

The turrets at either end stood out tall and clear, but the crenellations of the roofline looked like ocean waves due to irregularities in the old, uneven glass. The family coat of arms waved proudly in the breeze, announcing that Lord Hersham was in residence. Miranda's own likeness, closer to the window pane, was life-size, with the castle forming a background in the mirrored image. Her face was a pale oval, with two big, dark circles for eyes. An air bubble in the glass gave the illusion of a perfect teardrop on her cheek, but her eyes were dry. She was beyond tears.

As the present was so painful, she allowed her mind to return to the past, to the beginning of her adventure at Ashmead. She had come down to dinner that evening wearing the jonquil Italian crape gown Trudie had given her. Trudie found its pale color did not suit a blonde, but it looked well with Miranda's raven hair and dark eyes. It lent her an

4

unaccustomed air of elegance. In honor of the visit, she had bound her curls up in silver ribbons.

"By Jove, I will be falling in love with you if you don't watch out," Pavel had said jokingly.

That he said it in a loud voice in front of his parents and the rest of the company was as good as saying he did not mean it. How could Mama think Pavel would fall in love with her when they had been friends forever? Besides, he was not at all handsome and dashing like Rotham. At eighteen years, Miranda's own age, Pavel was a lanky, ungainly boy with a sad tendency to bump into furniture and trip over carpets. He still had a few spots, but even if he had been an Adonis, there would have been no romance. She had beaten him in too many races, both on foot and on horseback, for him to consider her a potential bride. She had even given him a nosebleed and seen him cry. He was like a brother.

"What a slow top you are, Pavel," a lazy, sardonic voice had drawled. "Not in love with Sissie yet after all these years of opportunity? I expected to hear wedding bells ere now. I am half in love with her already. Take care or I shall steal her from you."

It was Rotham who spoke, of course. Turning, Miranda had seen him lounging elegantly at the fireplace, one booted foot on the fender. He had just arrived and had not dressed for dinner. Obviously he did not intend to, but that was Rotham all over. He cared nothing for propriety. Although he had just completed a long journey, neither his blue jacket nor his fawn trousers showed any sign of dishevelment. His black hair shone like ebony in the lamplight. A satirical smile sat lightly on his handsome face as his dark eyes raked her from head to toe.

"Oh, you are back," she had said, rather irritably. She did not enjoy being teased in front of people.

A pair of well-arched eyebrows rose in mock dismay. "Is that any way to greet a hero, freshly returned from the trials of the great Congress of Vienna? You would not believe the hardships I have suffered. Nine-course banquets every evening—sometimes two an evening. Waltzing till dawn with the very diamonds of Continental Society, masques, plays, ridottos, and concerts past numbering. To say nothing of the flirtations." He raised two well-manicured fingers to conceal a yawn. "I feel as if I had accompanied the late Pheidippides on his jaunt from Athens to Sparta."

"Is there any news of Napoleon?" Miranda asked, feigning indifference to this enviable list of delights.

"He is still at large, still advancing inexorably toward Paris, gathering strength as he goes. Nothing succeeds like success. And though you forgot to inquire for the state of my health, Sissie, I am happy to be able to assure you I am fine."

Lady Hersham scowled at her son. "Is there any danger Boney will root out King Louis?" she asked.

"There is no saying with Napoleon," Rotham replied. He did not try to pull off his teasing stunts with his mama. She was not the sort of lady to tolerate it. "The Royalists went over to him at Grenoble, the same at Lyon. Louis has fled Paris. The *on dit* is that the servants are changing the flags at Fontainebleau in hourly expectation of the emperor's return."

"*Quelle désastre!*" the Comtesse Pierre de Valdor

6

exclaimed, with a flutter of her white hands. "What of your great Wellington?"

"He has alerted troops in the Low Countries," Rotham replied.

The comtesse's husband had been killed in a mysterious accident two years before. It was hinted, though never made entirely clear, that he had been engaged in some espionage business for King Louis. Since his death the comtesse had been a guest of the Hershams. She was a second cousin of Lady Hersham. It seemed strange that she spoke with a French accent, as she had been born and raised in England and had, in fact, never been off the island. Trudie had told Miranda it was an affectation adopted after the comte's death as it proved an effective aphrodisiac with English gentlemen. It sounded quite natural to Miranda as she had not known Louise when she spoke proper English, before marrying Comte Pierre.

The discussion turned to the doings of Bonaparte, with the comtesse expressing her wrath at this Corsican upstart. She had hoped to regain her late husband's castle in the Loire Valley when Louis was returned to the throne. "Vineyards of the most magnificent, Rotham," she explained. "Our Chenin Blanc makes a wine that holds its taste for a hundred years. You would adore the Château Valdor."

"I would adore any place where you are, Louise," he said with an exquisite bow. "Ça va sans dire. Whether I shall ever see those vineyards is a moot point. There is no denying Napoleon Bonaparte is the greatest Frenchman of his age, perhaps of any age. I suggest you cultivate a taste for sherry."

"He is not a Frenchman, that one!" the comtesse

exclaimed. "Corsican upstart! He is no more French than—"

"Than you?" Rotham suggested mischievously.

"I am French by marriage," she laughed, but with an angry sparkle in her green eyes. "A good wife always assumes her husband's nationality, along with his name, *n'est-ce pas?*"

"C'est vrai," he smiled, "and with just a little work, you will also assume the proper accent. Charming."

Despite his jibes, Rotham's doting smile made clear that he found no real flaw in the comtesse. Pavel also admired her. Nor were her conquests limited to gentlemen. Miranda thought she was the most glamorous female she had ever seen. She was cool, she was charming. She could tease and flirt one minute, and the next minute she would be gazing soulfully into space, thinking of Pierre. A deep sigh alerted the comtesse's audience that she now required a moment to remember.

Louise spoke of being "poor as a church mice"— fracturing English clichés was one of her linguistic skills—but she certainly did not look poor. She possessed an enviable wardrobe. Like a Frenchwoman born, she had found "a little French modiste" who dressed her in the highest kick of fashion for mere pennies. The various jewels that decked her white satin throat had been smuggled out of France sewn in the lining of Pierre's coat. His mama had thoughtfully arranged this before she and her comte were carried off to the guillotine.

Louise had a younger brother-in-law whom Miranda considered a potential husband. The Comte Laurent de Valdor—it seemed all the sons of a comte were called comte—did not actually make

8

his home with the Hershams, but he visited them so often, and for such lengthy periods, that it was a mere courtesy to call him a guest. He was at Ashmead that June, waiting to hear from London about a position as curator of the French collection at the British Museum.

"Watch out for Laurent," Trudie had warned her, which was an excellent goad to romance. "His pockets are to let. He might decide to marry your ten thousand, Miranda. Though, of course, he is the heir to Château Valdor now that Comte Pierre is dead, so perhaps he is worth keeping on the string."

Thus far he had shown little interest in her or her dot. Like Pavel and Rotham, he was a member of Louise's court. Miranda reluctantly admitted that the pair were admirably matched. Both so handsome. Comte Laurent's black hair and sultry eyes provided a magnificent contrast to Louise's golden curls and green eyes. Her vivacious, Gallic manner enlivened his brooding austerity.

The party took on a more staid tone when Lord Hersham joined the group in the Blue Saloon. He was a tall, lean gentleman whose face was lined from the rigors of keeping Rotham in check.

"So you are back, Rotham," he said, with no evidence of pleasure. "What news from Vienna?"

Rotham abandoned his lounging position and went to shake his papa's hand. His graceful motion revealed a set of broad shoulders, a lean body, and a strong, well-muscled leg. Miranda, sitting near the doorway, overheard Rotham's reply, although it was delivered in a confidential tone.

"I must speak to you, Papa. An urgent matter—"

"Boney has not beaten us?" Hersham asked sharply.

"No, no. It is not so serious as that."

Boxer, the butler, a comfortably padded man of middle years, appeared at the door and announced, "Dinner is served."

"Can it wait until after dinner?" Hersham asked his son.

"Yes, of course."

"My study. We shall skip port this evening. I take it you want privacy for this discussion?"

"The utmost privacy."

Hersham's face was grave as he gave Lady Hersham his arm to lead the procession to the dining room. Rotham accompanied the comtesse. Miranda found herself in the unusual position of having two gentlemen waiting on her. Pavel beat the comte to her side, and the comte followed in behind them. She always wished, when she went to the dining room, that Lady Hersham had chosen some other tapestry than the hunt to decorate the room. That pack of hounds, forever lunging for the poor fox's throat, always robbed her of appetite.

"I say, Sissie," Pavel said in a lowered voice as he held her chair, "did you hear what Rotham said to Papa? There is something afoot. I wager Boney has won the war, only Rotham don't want to upset the ladies."

"No, it is not that. Your papa asked him."

"What can it be?"

"I have no idea." They exchanged a look of mutual understanding.

"Right, we shall listen at the keyhole after dinner. Make some excuse to leave Mama and Louise and meet me in the library. I wonder if it has something to do with that trunk Rotham had taken up to his room. I heard him tell his valet to lock his bedroom door. Rotham never locks his door. I shall try to get hold of Cook's key chain and have a look. It's rather exciting, ain't it?"

"Yes."

It was always exciting at Ashmead, especially when Rotham was at home. Miranda had been sorry when he had not offered for Trudie. She thought he would have made an excellent brother-in-law—a terrible husband, with his flirting ways, but an excellent brother-in-law.

Chapter Two

Lady Hersham set an elegant table. Such a quantity of silver, crystal, and fine china were only brought out for special occasions at Wildwood, Miranda's home. A simple family dinner at Ashmead was always like a party.

The talk was by no means festive, however. They discussed the Congress of Vienna. The comtesse regretted that she had not been there.

"I have so many friends who would have been happy to give me rack and manger," she said. Then she recalled her dead husband and required a moment's silent gazing at the horrid tapestry. "I do not regret missing the parties—*mais non!*" she continued. "Only the chance to wind Talleyrand's ear and recover the family estate."

"Heh heh, I think you mean *bend* his ear, Louise," Pavel said, on cue. He had elected himself her official interpreter.

"But yes! That is my meaning *précisément.*" She smiled.

Rotham's eyes narrowed in interest. "The Congress is not over," he said. "You might get a tweak at Talleyrand's ear yet, Louise."

Lord Hersham gave him a damping look. "Don't be an ass, Rotham. Louise cannot go now, when it is four pence to a groat the cannons are roaring already. Boney may even win—there is no saying."

Comte Laurent scowled; the comtesse clutched her heart and gasped, "Do not say such things, *mon cher cousin*. He must not win."

"Of course he will not win," Lady Hersham announced. "Still, there is no point sticking our heads in the sand. There will be fighting in Europe. If Louise finds it a trifle dull here in the country—"

Louise took instant objection to this. "*Pas du tout!* I adore the little lambses and cow. So—how you say—bucolic?"

"What did you have in mind, Mary?" Lord Hersham asked his wife. He was not amused by the comtesse's annoying manner of speech, nor indeed by anything else about her, especially her proximity to his extremely eligible son and heir. His wife knew it well; they thought as one on this matter.

"I thought Louise might like to use the Brighton house for a few months," Lady Hersham replied. The comtesse's eyes lit up like a bonfire. "Brighton should be lively in this season, and the house is standing empty, since Rotham has taken up this Congress business. You *will* be remaining in London, Rotham?" she asked. It had just occurred to her she might be tossing her eldest son to this enticing she-wolf.

"I am to report to Castlereagh," Rotham replied. "I doubt I will find time to get to Brighton this year. There will be reams of paperwork, whichever way the business in Europe goes."

"Would you like to go to Brighton, Louise?" Lady Hersham asked hopefully.

"Happy as I am here at your lovely Ashmead, I do enjoy a change. Variety is the herb of life, *non*?"

She did not wait for Pavel to interpret but continued. "Brighton would be charming in summer. Right on the coast, so near to my beloved France. The Prince of Wales summers in Brighton, I believe?"

"I hope he does," Hersham said testily. "If he does not use that Xanadu pavilion of his in summer, I should like to know why we were put to the expense of building it. Dashed spendthrift. Shall I write and ask the Barges to open the house up, Comtesse? We leave the Barges there year-round to keep an eye on things."

"So kind," the comtesse said, her great green eyes misting with tears. "You are the bestest cousins a lady could have." She rose from her seat and went to place a modest kiss on Hersham's cheek.

Hersham did not employ his napkin to wipe away the kiss, but he looked as if he would like to.

"Harumph. Not at all. The place is standing idle," he said curtly. "Take the comte with you. You will want a man about the place. No impropriety in it, eh, Mary?" he said, rather commandingly, to his wife. "Just Laurent after all, a brother-in-law. The Barges will be there to play propriety."

The comte did not look entirely happy with this, perhaps because it suggested he was no threat to the lady's virtue.

"I shall hire a chaperon," he said.

"No need to hire one," the comtesse said at once. "Madame Lafleur would enjoy a little holiday by the sea. You permit, Lady Hersham?"

"Excellent, the very thing. Take Madame Lafleur with you by all means."

"Who is Madame Lafleur?" Hersham inquired.

"A friend from Rye," the comtesse replied.

"That Frenchie who bought Tadwell's little cottage," Pavel added. "She and Louise are close as inkle weavers—because of being French, you know. Madame Lafleur has no family. She lives like a hermit, except for seeing Louise and Laurent."

"She is a Royalist, *Ça va sans dire,*" the comtesse added hastily. "The family were friends and neighbors of the Valdors in France, before the troubles."

Details of the visit were discussed during dinner. Miranda was sorry to hear that Laurent would be leaving Ashmead. The comtesse's main concern was that she must get to the village, *aussitôt que possible*, to order a new summer gown from Mademoiselle Chêne, her modiste. As soon as dinner was over, the ladies rose to leave the gentlemen to their port.

"You must forgive us, Comte," Hersham said to Laurent. "Rotham and I have some business to discuss. Pavel will bear you company."

As soon as Hersham and Rotham left, Pavel excused himself, leaving Laurent alone. "I have promised to show Miss Miranda my—a book," he said, and rushed from the room.

Laurent poured himself a glass of his lordship's excellent port, lit one of his fine cheroots, and settled back to consider the summer with Louise and Madame Lafleur at Brighton. A smile of anticipation softened the harsh contours of his handsome face.

Miranda had no difficulty escaping the Blue Saloon. The comtesse had her nose buried in the latest copy of *La Belle Assemblée*, and Lady Hersham was having her usual postprandial snooze by the grate. When Miranda heard the gentle snorts begin to issue from her hostess's nostrils, she excused herself and darted to the library, where Pavel was waiting.

"Papa just closed the door," he said, with a knowing look. "He don't usually bother. Let us go and eavesdrop."

They tiptoed down the hallway to the oak-paneled doorway of Lord Hersham's study. The door was stout, but as the voice within was raised to an alarming degree, it was possible to overhear part of the discussion.

"You did *what!*" Lord Hersham bellowed, in horrified accents.

Rotham's reply, uttered in apologetic tones, was a mere mumble.

"Good God! Are you mad? You will be the death of me yet with your freakish starts. Have you no common sense, no common decency? You have brought disgrace on the name of Hersham. I am ashamed to call you my son. Were you foxed?"

"A trifle bosky, but—" The rest was inaudible.

Pavel and Miranda exchanged a look of amazement. "He has gone and got some woman enceinte," Pavel said, more in envy than disgust. "I wonder who she is."

They both applied their ears to the oak again. "That could be a hanging matter," Hersham said. "It is particularly dangerous with Boney on the loose again."

This did not sound like getting some wench pregnant to Miranda. She stared at Pavel. "Surely he has not been carrying on with Bonaparte's wife! Marie-Louise is at Vienna, is she not?"

"But that is precisely why I took it!" Rotham said.

Pavel frowned. "Sounds as if he stole something.

What could it be? I wager it is in that trunk he had locked in his room."

"You must put it back at once, Rotham," Hersham said angrily. "Rash of you. If anyone ever found out—"

"You must not tell a soul, Papa. I had to tell someone. I wanted your advice. You have always helped me in the past."

This flattery mollified Hersham somewhat. "Naturally you may count on my discretion. A pity I could not count on yours. Is it really— Let me have another look."

After a silence, Hersham continued. "Can you not get it smuggled back to France immediately? No one need ever know you took it."

"I haven't time. Castlereagh wants me in London."

"Does he know?"

"Not yet. Do you think I ought to tell him?"

"Write him this very night. He'll know what is best to be done. No fear of his spreading the tale."

Pavel said in a low voice, "It cannot be silk, as I first thought. Louise asked him to bring her back some silk if he could get hold of it. There is no point searching his room. Whatever it is, he has it in there, showing it to Papa. Perhaps we can get a peek after they leave."

"Could it be the crown jewels of France?" Miranda suggested. She knew Rotham held nothing sacred. He had once mounted a pulpit in a church in Brighton and delivered a sermon, pretending to be a visiting vicar. It had gone over very well, too. "Your papa spoke of hanging. It must be something awfully important."

"It could be gold, I daresay."

17

"I doubt two footmen could carry a trunk full of gold. It would weigh a ton. They had no trouble getting the trunk upstairs, did they?"

"Devil a bit of it. Trotted it up as easily as if it were empty."

Hersham and Rotham remained closeted for an hour. After Hersham's first angry outbreak, the voices became more conciliating. At one point they even laughed.

"By God, it serves them right!" Hersham said. "Lifting it right out from under their noses. Mary will want to see this."

"Do you think it wise to show Mama?" Rotham asked in alarm.

"Your own mama is not likely to turn you over to the law. Of course she must see it. The chance of a lifetime."

Every utterance raised Miranda's curiosity a notch higher. What could it be? The sound of footfalls was heard approaching the study. Miranda and Pavel scampered back into the library. They listened at the doorway as Lady Hersham was summoned, then ran to the study to hear what she had to say. She did not seem to be much impressed at this once-in-a-lifetime viewing.

"A shabby-looking thing. I have seen better work than this in my own home," she said dismissingly.

"But it is very old," her husband pointed out.

"You have really outdone yourself this time, Rotham," Lady Hersham said. "Take it back, at once, before they send the gendarmes after you. Foolish boy."

The mystery was still unsolved when Lady Hersham returned to the Blue Saloon. Nor was it much clearer when the trunk was carried upstairs by Hersham and Rotham. That they did not ask the servants to carry it suggested Lord Hersham's idea of its importance. After they descended Pavel made a dart upstairs to just check and see that Rotham's door was locked. It was. He discovered by peeking through keyholes that Slack, Rotham's valet, was in the sitting room with his ears cocked as well.

Slack came to the doorway when he heard Pavel try the doorknob. "Can I help you, Lord Pavel?" he asked suspiciously. Slack was a dark-visaged, wiry fellow, so devoted to his master that he had forsaken all other pleasures in life. He had neither wife, mistress, nor friends. Looking after Lord Rotham was a full-time job.

"I was just looking for Rotham," Pavel replied.

"You will find his lordship belowstairs, sir."

They found him in the Blue Saloon, having a tête-à-tête with Louise. Behind them hung a French tapestry that just suited the lady. It featured beaux and belles at leisure, frolicking in front of a castle. Laurent, having returned from the dining room, was seated apart from the others, near a lamp to get light. He looked on jealously from the side of a journal he pretended to read. As the Hershams were not present, Miranda assumed they were back in the study, discussing whatever it was Rotham had stolen. Rotham was urging Louise to abandon the idea of Brighton and go to Vienna instead.

"You really ought to be there to put forward your claim to the Valdor estate," he urged.

Laurent's newspaper rustled irritably. The Château Valdor would be *his* one day, not Louise's.

The comtesse replied, "But if—how I hate to even

think it—if Bonaparte wins, then what is the point?"

"It is a beautiful trip this time of year, through France. There is no fighting there. I have just passed through it. The chestnut and lime trees are lovely. The inns are clean and cheap." He spoke on persuasively, "It is entirely peaceful. The fighting will be in the Low Countries. That is where Wellington speaks of meeting Boney. The war might drag on for months, there is no saying. And if Boney wins—when will you ever get to see France? Meanwhile, Vienna is as gay as if no one had ever heard of war."

"Are *you* returning?" she asked, with a knowing gaze.

"I will learn my fate after I have reported to Castlereagh. I shall try to get to Vienna."

The air crackled with innuendo as they exchanged a look.

"I could not go unescorted," she said.

"That is true, but I am sure you have many friends who would be happy to accompany you. Monsieur Berthier spoke of going to Vienna the last time I met him."

"That commoner! How can you suggest such a thing!"

"He is a stout Royalist, I think?"

"So he says. I could not travel with a bachelor, Rotham. That is not *comme il faut*."

"Not without a suitable chaperon, obviously. My thinking is that Berthier is a well-traveled gentleman. He could act as your courier."

Again Laurent's journal rustled in vexation. Why did Rotham not suggest the obvious—that he, the comte, accompany Louise?

"I doubt Berthier could afford the trip," Louise said. "Nor could I, come to that. It would be *très cher*," she added. Her sparkling green eyes asked a tacit question.

"Something could be arranged," Rotham replied. "Berthier is at Hythe at the moment, is he? I know he moves about a good deal."

"I do not keep a route of Berthier," she said.

Pavel, who had sauntered close to learn how to flirt, said, "I think you mean you do not keep track of him, Comtesse."

"Just so. Do you think I would be safe with Berthier?" she asked, returning her attention to Rotham.

"Surely the question is rather, would he be safe from the temptation you provide?" His eyes slid slowly from her face down to her décolletage.

She preened in pleasure. "I could not tempt a monk in this old rag," she said. "What are the ladies in Vienna wearing this spring, Rotham?"

"None of them can touch you, *ma chere Louise*," he replied. "But if you wish to cut a swath, I brought home some rather pretty silks. I have them in my trunk. I thought of your *beaux yeux* when I bought the emerald green—and several other times as well."

"It is silks you have in that black trunk then, is it, Rotham?" Pavel asked. "I wondered at your bringing home an extra trunk."

Rotham stiffened in annoyance. He heard the ironic edge to his brother's voice. He noticed that the Vale chit had both ears cocked as well. Surely they hadn't gotten into his trunk? No, it was impossible. Slack had guarded it every minute.

"Among other things," he answered nonchalantly.

21

"I also brought you back some lead soldiers for your collection, Pavel."

"Did you, by Jove?" Pavel exclaimed, still young enough to be diverted by this treat. "I hope they are cavalry officers."

"Some of the officers are mounted on horses." He turned to Miranda. "And last, but by no means least, you must choose an ell of silk as well, Sissie," he said. "I see you in brighter colors. That is not to denigrate your yellow gown, but you raven-haired beauties do marvelous things to rich colors."

His eyes made a practiced sweep of Miranda from head to toe. When had little Sissie Vale grown into such a beauty? Her ivory skin was just tinged with rose, high on the full cheeks. A light dusting of freckles over her nose added a provincial touch that pleased him. She wore her black hair swept simply back from her brow, to tumble in a riot of curls behind. Her figure was coming along nicely. He had always felt she had great promise; now it seemed that promise was coming to fulfillment. But why was she glowering so? It was his little flirtation with Louise, no doubt. He hoped she was not going to be a prude, like her sister. She took the shine out of Trudie. But then Rotham had always favored dark-haired girls.

Miranda felt again that flare of annoyance at being examined by this acknowledged rake. His eyes burned into her like live coals. He had broken Trudie's heart, but he would not touch hers.

"I already have enough gowns, thank you," she replied coolly.

His eyebrows rose in astonishment. "I must congratulate you. You are unique in all of Christendom. When did a lady ever have enough gowns?"

"Trudie gives me all her old ones," she replied with childlike candor. "Not worn out, but ones she no longer cares for. She gave me this one. It is real Italian crape," she boasted, holding up the skirt for him to admire the material. "She only had it a month. Parnham did not care for it."

"Parnham must be blind," Rotham murmured, with a last appreciative examination of the gown, and the lithe body in it. Then his eyes lifted to see her pretty face scowling at him. A farouche little creature. She should be taught some manners.

"He is fussy about what colors Trudie wears," she said. "He likes her best in blue, to match her eyes."

"How unimaginative. Just like Parnham. We cannot deck you in gray, to match your eyes, however. I have a nice bolt of rose. . . ." He mentally dressed her in a deeper color to do justice to that raven hair. It shimmered amber and rose and peacock blue in the flames from the grate. She could wear any color—she would even look well in the dreary white gowns of a deb, when she made her curtsey at St. James's next year in London.

"I already said I do not want any," she said sharply. Then she added, "Thank you all the same. When are you going to London?"

"Soon. Will you miss me?" he asked flirtatiously, as it obviously annoyed her. He expected another scowl and was surprised when she gave a pert grin.

"But of course I shall! There are no parties at Ashmead when you are not here."

He smiled, unfazed. "Out of the mouths of babes! There is nothing so incredible—and disheartening —as the bald truth. I am a mere provider of entertainment, just one step up from a Punch and Judy showman. Now that you have put up your hair and let down your skirts, you must learn the civil way to entertain a gentleman. I recommend the gentle art of flattery, even when it involves telling a lie." He turned to Louise. "Now there is a project you might undertake, Louise, licking Sissie into shape."

Louise gave him a disparaging look. "I do not traffic in lies and flatteries, milord. Miss Miranda deals very well with gentlemen her own age. She is too young to learn how to deal with a *vieillard* like you. Let the child be."

Miranda gave the comtesse a baleful stare that went unnoticed. The comtesse could always make her feel lumpish and young, but to be called a child only because she told the truth!

Rotham considered this advice a moment, then said, "To show my generosity, you will both have a reward for putting me in my place. The green silk for you, Louise, and a party for Sissie before I leave, so that she will remember me when I am gone, and hopefully regret her harsh words. Cut to the quick!"

Miranda fixed him with a gimlet eye. With a thought of the trunk abovestairs, she said, "I thought you had to leave right away."

"Not right away, but soon. Pleasure before business has always been my motto. We shall throw together a rout for tomorrow evening. You must save me the first dance."

"You should stand up first with the comtesse," Miranda pointed out. "She has a title."

Rotham cast a teasing glance on the comtesse. "At least she did not say 'age before beauty,'" he said.

Louise jerked her shawl about her shoulders angrily. "Pierre was much older than I," she said. "Not that I care a twig about age."

"You mean a fig, Louise," Pavel said.

She did not reply, but she patted his hand to show her appreciation. "Pavel has the heart of a Frenchman," she said to Rotham. "In France, the gentlemen are more interested in a lady's mind than her age. French ladies care nothing for a wrinkle."

Rotham allowed his eyebrows to rise to his hair. "You have been misinformed, my pet. Your comprehensive knowledge of French customs is at fault. It has been my experience that, like the English and Austrian ladies, the *femmes* of France spend a disproportionate amount of time worrying about what their menfolk consider of only secondary importance, viz., keeping up an appearance of youth."

Louise lifted her hand to fluff out her hair. "Perhaps they are setting their *chapeaux* for Englishmen, milord."

"Your point, madam. One can only admire their intelligence; they insist on the best." Laurent rustled his newspaper impatiently to show his disgust with the conversation. Rotham called to him, "You are quite right, Laurent. Comparisons are odious. You are so quiet I forgot you are present."

Miranda rose to join Laurent as she felt it rude to ignore him entirely, and besides, this was an excellent opportunity to get to know him better.

Before leaving the group by the grate, she said to Rotham, "Are you really going to have a rout tomorrow evening? Because if you are, I shall have to send home for a gown."

"Yes, I am. Really." He rose to accompany her. "We English gentlemen are as good as our word. By

25

all means invite Trudie and her baron, if they are at Wildwood."

"No, they are not. Where did you get that idea?"

"You mentioned Trudie giving you the gown."

"She gave it to me last winter."

"I see. One does not like to appear rude, and indeed I could not be happier that you are with us—an unexpected delight—but one does just wonder why you have removed to Ashmead, when your own home is only a mile away."

"Sukey has the measles."

"Ah, and you have come to share them with us. That is very kind of you."

"I do not have them. I was sent here so I would not become infected. Lady Hersham assured Mama that everyone here had had them already."

"I recall I had them at the same time as you did yourself. In fact, I blame you for infecting me. Is there a new strain that can be had twice? My last bout was—oh, five years ago?"

Miranda blushed at being caught out in a transparent ruse for being here. "Three. It was the spring you were making up to Trudie."

"Three." He nodded. "I was trying to teach you to jump a ditch. You were riding that Welsh pony."

"Mama thought perhaps that was chicken pox. She could not recall and thought it a wise precaution to send me here."

"Did you ever learn to jump the pony?"

"Yes, no thanks to you. You jilted Trudie after you got the measles."

"Or chicken pox, as the case may be."

Miranda wanted to have the last word. She said, "You were very rude to Laurent, saying that Frenchmen are no good."

26

"I did not say no good. I said not so good as Englishmen."

"That is a matter of opinion. I think they are much more interesting."

"And you only—what? Seventeen? Not old enough to appreciate their love of older women."

"I am eighteen."

"Still too young to cut your teeth on a wicked Frenchman, *ma petite*. I suggest you flirt with me instead."

Miranda felt some charm in his wicked dark eyes, which gazed admiringly at her. Rotham had never turned his charms on her before. She could never understand how all the local girls, one after the other, could make such cakes of themselves over him. She began to understand how he did it. He made you feel special, when he smiled at you like that, as if you were the only girl in the world. But she knew how evanescent his romances were, and how long and painful the cure.

She studied him with a frank, unemotional stare. "I think you must be about the most wicked man in England," she said. "I shall stick to Frenchmen." Then she left him and joined Laurent.

Rotham stood looking after her, admiring her tiny waist and the gentle, feminine sway of her hips. One black curl had escaped its ribbon and nestled enticingly on the nape of her neck. Now there was a facer! He really would have to teach the chit some manners. He looked forward to it with a familiar stirring of excitement.

Chapter Three

The comte had all the qualifications of an excellent flirt. He was handsome, he was some years older than Miranda, a man of the world, he was French with a charming trace of accent, a relative stranger to her, and she had been warned away from him. But after a quarter of an hour's uphill work, she decided he was unflirtable.

When asked his opinion of Bonaparte's escape, he said, "The man ought to have been shot when they had the chance. Mad dogs are incurable. There will be no peace in France while he lives. He is as bad as the revolutionaries. You will see, mademoiselle, my family estate will be given to some general or jumped-up bureaucrat. The Valdors have lived in the Loire Valley for three hundred years, but we will live there no more. Talleyrand is our only hope, and he is a sly dog when all is said and done. His allegiance is with King Louis at the moment. You are aware of his principle of legitimacy, of course, that restored the throne to Louis."

"I have heard of it," she lied.

"Bah! If Talleyrand thinks Bonaparte will succeed, you will see the chameleon change his skin once again. He held a high position in the French Revolution, he worked for Bonaparte, now he claims to be on the king's side. Whatever befalls the rest of us, Talleyrand will end up on his feet. I cannot trust the man."

This was a little too much politics for Miranda. She said, "It is very vexing, to be sure, but there is little you can do about it. You must try to enjoy Brighton. It is lovely at this time of the year."

"I shall not go to Brighton if the comtesse goes to Austria. Why does Lord Rotham push this dangerous scheme on her? It is because he plans to return himself." A flush suffused his swarthy cheeks. "I am the head of my family now," he said. "It is for me to protect her. I shall forbid the trip. *C'est tout.*"

"I do think it dangerous," she agreed, and tried once more to steer the conversation into more sociable channels. "Lord Rotham is having a rout tomorrow evening," she said.

"A rout! When Europe is on the very edge of collapse! Has the man never heard of Nero, fiddling while Rome burns? Why does he linger here? Why does he not fly, *ventre à terre*, to London to arrange matters with Lord Castlereagh? It was a gross error to send Castlereagh away from Austria at this time. Wellington is a general; I have never heard he is a statesman."

Miranda looked regretfully to the grate, where the others were enjoying themselves. Rotham had brought in a large wicker basket and was showing Louise the silks. Pavel was already arranging his lead soldiers on the sofa. Laurent looked to the grate as well.

"Rotham said the silks were in his trunk," he said. "The shabby black trunk he had taken to his room."

Miranda said, "Perhaps he put them in the wicker

basket to bring them downstairs," although she did not believe it. Or at least she did not believe the silks had come from the black trunk.

"No, the wicker basket was left with the butler." He gave a conscious look, as though he regretted his words. "I happened to notice, when he came in," he added.

"I expect he had his clothes in the trunk."

"Very likely," Laurent said. But he knew very well that Rotham had told his man to lock that trunk in his room and guard it with his life. He had just entered the Blue Saloon when Rotham arrived and had overheard the order. Laurent had seen the two trunks being carried abovestairs. A man did not lock his clothes in his room and set a guard on them—although he would like to steal one of those dashing jackets. Weston! Ah, the man was a magician.

Laurent was convinced there were orders for Castlereagh in the trunk, and he was passionately curious to see them. It was disgraceful the way these politicians managed matters among themselves, as though they were the lords of creation, and the rest of the population were their pawns. Disgraceful, too, the way Rotham was flirting with Louise.

"You would like to admire the silks, *non?*" he said to Miranda, for he wished to join the other group himself and planned to use her as an excuse.

"Yes, let us have a look," she agreed at once, and escaped from the dour Frenchman. She did not despise his seriousness. Quite the contrary, she admired his interest in serious matters, but she had thought a Frenchman would realize that a tête-à-tête was not the time or place to indulge in politics.

"This one. I shall take this one," Louise said, running her white hands possessively over an ell of emerald silk. She held it up to her face. Her green eyes echoed the emerald hue, and her golden curls provided an exciting contrast. "What do you think, Laurent?" she asked, with a provocative smile.

"*Ravissante,*" Laurent said softly, with a hungry look in his eyes.

Louise smiled and made a purring sound of pleasure. "I shall take it to Mademoiselle Chêne tomorrow and see how quickly she can make it up."

Rotham lifted an ell of rose silk from the basket. It fell from his fingers in a shimmering ripple with a light rustling sound. "Sissie, are you sure I cannot tempt you?" he asked.

She gazed longingly at the silk. "No, thank you," she said primly. "I expect you bought it for Selena. Why do you not give it to her?" Selena was Rotham's married sister.

He shrugged to conceal his annoyance. She wanted it all right; his experience with ladies told him so. What it did not tell him was why she should refuse. "I brought a blue bolt for Selena, but I doubt I shall have any trouble getting rid of the rose." He tossed the bolt carelessly aside.

Miranda assumed it would grace the back of one of his mistresses. She would keep an eye out for it in Rye.

There was a commotion at the doorway as Lord and Lady Hersham came in, accompanied by the tea tray. Louise poured, as Lady Hersham disliked the bother. The conversation turned to other matters. Rotham had been away for six weeks and had to be brought up to date on estate doings and local gossip. Lord Hersham looked surprised when his elder son informed him he planned to have a rout the next evening.

"You are putting off your trip to London, then?" he asked.

"There is a matter I have to take care of here first," Rotham replied. They exchanged a meaningful glance.

So did Miranda and Pavel. The battered black trunk with the padlock was on the minds of all four of them.

"It will take a deal of work to arrange a party in one day," Lady Hersham said. "I shall have a word with Cook, and perhaps you would begin making up a guest list, Sissie. You know who Rotham would like to invite. You must ask any of your friends as well, of course. I daresay this rout is in Sissie's honor, eh, Rotham?"

"Just so, Mama. Sissie tells me she did not miss me during my absence, but she did miss the parties. I took the hint."

"I was not hinting!" Miranda exclaimed, her cheeks flaming. Nor had she actually said she did not miss him. She had only implied she did not.

"There is no need to apologize," Lady Hersham said. "We are overdue for a little rout. A couple of dozen guests—we need not invite them for dinner first. You and Pavel can ride around tomorrow and deliver the cards."

"We shall write up the cards this evening," Miranda said. Her hand flew to her lips. "Oh, I was going to help you repair the tapestry tomorrow, Lady Hersham."

"Another few days will not do it much harm. It has been perishing for five hundred years."

After tea the group broke up. Rotham claimed he

had some correspondence to attend to. He went to his papa's study. Lord Hersham soon joined him there. Miranda and Pavel agreed to fill out the cards for the party in the library. Only Louise and Laurent remained by the fireside. Laurent looked very well pleased. As Miranda and Pavel departed, he joined Louise on the sofa.

It was to be only a small party, and the invitation cards were soon written. As he piled them into a stack, Pavel said, "I believe I shall nip down for a word with Cook."

"Your mama was going to do that," Miranda replied.

"Mama will be gone by now. She will only say, 'You know best what will be required, Cook,' and leave. I mean to visit the wine cellar, for an excuse to get hold of the house keys. Cook has a key to the cellars. It put Boxer's nose out of joint when Papa gave her one. Serves the butler right. He will insist on keeping even the cooking sherry locked up. I shall slip the key to Rotham's room off the ring and see if we can get a look at the trunk. Cook will never notice the key is gone."

"Laurent is interested in the trunk," Miranda said.

"Is he? It was kind of you to try to entertain him. All you got for your efforts was another tirade, I daresay?"

"Yes, he is very worried about Bonaparte."

"He is a dead bore. He thinks he knows it all, but you don't see him stirring a finger to help out against Boney. Sitting on his backside, waiting for Rotham and the rest of them to handle the job, then he will complain some more."

"He is unhappy," Miranda said forgivingly.

"Then he ought to get a job."

"You know he is trying, Pavel. I hope he gets that position at the British Museum."

"So do I! I am sick of his thundercloud of a face."

"He is very handsome." She sighed.

"I suppose that means you have a *tendre* for him. Waste of time, m'dear. He has eyes for no one but Louise."

"She will never marry a penniless man. I daresay that is why he is so eager to reclaim his ancestral home."

"Until he does get it back, you would do better to keep away from him, or he will end up with your ten thousand in his pocket. Are you coming with me to the kitchen?"

"Of course."

As they went into the hallway, they saw someone—a man—just peeling around the corner.

"Who was that? I wonder if he was listening at the door!" Miranda exclaimed.

"Probably a footman," Pavel said, with little interest, and continued to the kitchen.

Cook handed over the keys with no trouble. She also provided a candle for them to go to the cellar. It was a vast, damp, dark, cool cavern, holding bins of root vegetables in the first room, with the wine in the next chamber. They did not move beyond the root cellar. While Miranda held the candle, Pavel searched the ring for the key to Rotham's room.

"I know it is number seventeen," he said, "for he used to keep pictures of scantily clad women under his mattress when he was young. He used to lock his door then. It took me half an hour to find out which key was his. Now that is deuced odd!" he exclaimed, fingering the keys. "Number seventeen is

34

missing! He took the spare key! By Jove, whatever he is hiding, it must be worth seeing."

"What a take-in. Let us go upstairs. There are horrid black beetles on the floor here."

They scampered back up to the kitchen. Pavel got Cook aside and said in a knowing way as he handed her the keys, "Rotham got his key from you all right, did he?"

"Oh yes, milord. I gave it to Slack this very afternoon, soon as they arrived. Slack took the key for the sitting room as well, as there is no key for the door between the rooms. You need have no fear foreigners will see that dispatch from Austria." She nodded her head in a conspiratorial fashion.

So that was the story Slack had used for secrecy. As if a dispatch required a whole trunk. "Good work," Pavel said.

"What wine will you be wanting for tomorrow night, then?"

He gave a start of surprise, for he had forgotten all about the wine. "The usual," he said. "I see there is no shortage. Just tell Boxer to bring up the usual. There will be twenty-four guests."

When he and Miranda left, he said, "Rotham had Slack get the key the minute he arrived. And the key to the sitting room as well. What the devil can be so important that he wants no one to see it?"

"It cannot be more pictures of naked women, or he would not have shown them to Hersham. I have no idea," she said.

"Nor have I, but tomorrow while the rout is on, I mean to get into that room, if I have to tear down a wall to do it."

"Is there a vine outside his window?" Miranda asked.

"No, just that old oak tree, and it is more than twenty feet from the house. You would have to be an ape to leap it."

"What about a ladder? Does Rotham leave his window open?"

"Yes, by Jove! He does in weather like this. He is a demon for fresh air. Right. We'll get out the ladder tomorrow night while Rotham is busy flirting with Louise at the rout."

This sounded entirely satisfactory to Miranda. With an exciting day ahead of her, she retired early to her room. Her bedchamber, like most of the spaces at Ashmead, displayed a tapestry on the windowless wall. It was called *The Virgin and the Unicorn* and pictured a medieval lady wearing what looked like a dunce's pointed hat. She stood on a chamomile lawn, guarded by a unicorn wearing a blue cape on one side and a tiger similarly arrayed on the other. Smaller animals—rabbits and dogs mostly— disported themselves on the grass. The colors had faded to delicate pastels over the centuries.

Lady Hersham had told her a unicorn was a mythical wild animal that could only be captured by a virgin. Miranda thought it a silly story, but the tapestry was pretty. Not all the older tapestries at Ashmead were so nice. Many of them had religious themes, as it was mainly the church that could afford tapestries during the Middle Ages. They were placed in churches and convents. The aristocracy also commissioned some, but most of them had been lost or destroyed as they were carried about on the Crusades and used roughly. The gold threads had been pulled out and melted down. The few that survived were shabby beyond repair.

Lady Hersham was very fond of her tapestries.

"There is no finer private collection in all of England," she would say proudly. Miranda heard an echo of the lady's voice inside her head. "I have seen better work than this in my own home," she had said, when she was looking at the secret in Rotham's trunk. Was it a tapestry he had stolen? The trunk was the right size for a small tapestry, but surely a stolen tapestry was not a hanging matter, not for a peer of the realm. It was said to be particularly dangerous with Boney on the loose. Boney was not an aficionado of tapestries, was he?

Why had Hersham wanted his wife to see the secret? He would not call her to view secret documents. Nor would she proclaim them "a shabby-looking thing." It was a great mystery, but as Miranda gazed with unfocused eyes at the unicorn, it was not of the secret that she thought. It was of Rotham, offering her the rose silk and suggesting she flirt with him. A lady would have to be a fool to flirt with a rake. He was no unicorn, to be captured by a virgin. Louise was more his style, and she was welcome to him. They would probably meet in Vienna, away from the family, and have a madly passionate affair. That would leave poor Laurent heartbroken.

Chapter Four

Miranda awoke to the raucous call of a bluejay beyond her window, accompanied by the less strident but pitiful chirping of the bird whose nest the jaw was attacking. She rose and threw open the mullioned window. Seeing the situation, she threw one of a pair of brass candlesticks into the tree. The jay flew off, only to perch brazenly on the next tree, preparing to attack again. Miranda took aim with the other candlestick and nearly hit the jay. It flew off with an angry caw, at least temporarily routed. She must remember to retrieve the candlesticks after breakfast. They were already old and dented, so she did not fear she had destroyed them.

The French clock on the dresser told her it was only eight o'clock, but in June it looked like midmorning—a beautiful morning. The sun shone in an azure sky, with little puffs of white cotton clouds floating high above. Glancing at the tapestry, she smiled at the unicorn. Even a unicorn seemed possible on such a day as this.

Too impatient to wait for warm water, she poured the cold water in the pitcher into the basin and made a hasty ablution before dressing. As the day was so fine, she wore her pink sprigged muslin gown and drew her hair carelessly back with a pink ribbon. A few wayward curls tumbled forward over her cheeks. Her mind was not on her toilette. All she could think of was that there was a delightful mystery waiting to be solved at Ashmead Hall, and a rout party this evening. She was in the dining room by eight-fifteen, where she found an impatient Pavel waiting for her. No one else was at table. Hersham would be up and about already.

"Sleepyhead! What kept you?" he grumbled. "We have to work out a plan." He had already breakfasted and was sipping coffee.

While Miranda helped herself to gammon and eggs from the tempting array at the sideboard, she said, "We also have to deliver the cards for the rout party."

Pavel ignored this detail. "I have been examining Rotham's window. It is open right enough, but how are we to get Slack out of the room long enough to get inside? We require a distraction."

"Does he like a tipple?" Miranda asked. "We might put some laudanum in a bottle of wine."

"Slack is sober as a Methodist."

"Oh. Perhaps I could create a diversion to draw him out into the hallway while you get in by the window." She took her plate to the table and began eating breakfast.

"An excellent idea, but do not think you can flirt him into abandoning his post. Rotham would turn him off if he found him flirting with a guest."

"I might pretend to have fainted. He would have to come to my assistance. I could ask him to accompany me to my room. He could hardly refuse."

"You will have to make a racket to catch his attention. Fall, or—I have it! You could pretend you saw the ghost and give a good loud shriek. The upstairs maid sees the Blue Lady often at the top of the stairs, just steps from Rotham's room."

"Excellent! We must choose a time when Rotham is not about," Miranda said. "Tonight, while he is busy at the rout would be best."

"I have got the ladder close to the house, hidden behind the yews. Oh, I picked up the candlesticks while I was about it. Why did you pitch them out the window? Did you catch someone snooping?" he asked hopefully.

"No, just a marauding bluejay."

"You was too late. There were two broken robin eggs beneath the tree. Dashed bluejays. I shall get out my gun when I have a moment free."

Miranda made a hasty breakfast, and they were off—in a lowly whisky, alas, drawn by a pony.

"Papa is using his carriage this morning," Pavel said, "and there is no point asking Rotham for the use of his curricle. He will allow no one but himself to hold the ribbons of his famous grays. Besides, he mentioned going to Hythe. It would be an excellent time to get into his room, except that Slack will be there."

"I wonder why he is going to Hythe," Miranda said, frowning.

"Nothing to do with the trunk. I asked him. He promised Castlereagh to take him a barrel of brandy. He will be speaking to Andy Macpherson. He runs the smuggling at Hythe."

Supplying the foreign secretary of England with contraband cargo was an unexceptionable explanation for Rotham's trip. Miranda gathered up the invitations, put on her bonnet, and they began their drive. By setting out early they found all their invitees at home, though not all of them were up and about at such a farouche hour. They saved the invitations for Rye for the last.

This hilly town, clinging to a bulge of red sandstone that protruded from Romney Marsh, offered hard walking. They kept the whisky until they had delivered the invitations. It was understood without saying that they would go on the strut on the High Street after. They stabled the gig at the Mermaid Hotel, then went poking about the everything shop. Pavel bought two inferior tin soldiers, and Miranda fell victim to a string of glass beads. They enjoyed a refreshing ice as they climbed to the hilltop, looking over the polder and the sea beyond.

It was when they were returning to the Mermaid that Miranda espied Laurent. As he had shown interest in the black trunk, they decided to follow him. He was walking, which was strange as Rye was some five miles from Ashmead. How had he gotten here? They followed him along the High Street at a discreet distance. At Conduit Hill he left the High Street. Their question was soon answered. Louise's carriage was standing outside Mademoiselle Chêne's modiste shop. Laurent was obviously going to meet her.

"Mademoiselle is making her green gown for Brighton," Miranda said, with a wistful thought of the rose silk.

"And Laurent is trailing at her apron strings as usual, the gudgeon," Pavel added.

Louise and Laurent, engrossed in conversation, did not notice the youngsters lurking across the street when they came out of the modiste's shop. They proceeded down the block to Madame Lafleur's in Louise's carriage. This, too, was an innocent visit. Madame Lafleur was to chaperon the

41

Valdors at Brighton. Finding no further clues, Pavel suggested they return to the Mermaid. They passed the milliner's shop, Madame Arouet's, on the way. It struck Miranda that half the shops in Rye had French names. When had the French performed this peaceful invasion?

Intrigued by this suspicious surfeit of French names, she did not observe the tall gentleman advancing toward them. It was Pavel's exclamation that caused her to look up and spot him. There was no denying Rotham was a highly polished article. He took the shine out of all the local bucks, with his exquisitely tailored jackets and his shining Hessians. His very stride, long and bold, bespoke a gentleman who knew he was cock of the walk. When he drew to a stop to speak to them, she felt a little thrill.

"What brings you two to Rye?" he asked, but his dark eyes looked only at Miranda. Little Sissie looked enchanting in her chipped straw bonnet and flowered muslin. Her youthful innocence was a refreshing change after the debauch going forth in Vienna. It had surprised even Rotham, and he was no provincial.

"We are delivering invitations to your rout," she replied.

"To *our* rout," he said. "You have forgotten so soon that it is being held in your honor? Were you thinking of giving an invitation to Mr. Belanger?" he asked, jokingly. It was in front of Belanger's Book and Stationery Shop that they met.

"No, I was just noticing how many French people there are in this town," she said. "Mademoiselle Chêne, Arouet's, Belanger's—and the Dumonts and Lefebvres, who are coming to your rout, Rotham."

"Nothing to do with Boney, if that is what you are getting at," Pavel told her. "It is ancient history. These folks are Huguenots, or some such thing."

"What are Huguenots?" she asked shamelessly.

"Something to do with religious persecution, was it not, Rotham?" he asked.

"I must have a word with your tutor," Rotham murmured, with a pained frown. "The Huguenots were French Protestants, who found sanctuary here in the sixteenth and seventeenth centuries. I believe we can acquit them of harboring anti-English sentiments as they have been here some hundreds of years. You ought to know what a Huguenot is, Pavel."

"Why should I lumber my head with that ancient stuff?"

"Mademoiselle Chêne has not been here that long," Miranda said. "And she is only a modiste, so she would not have been escaping from the Revolution."

"Lafleur is a newcomer as well," Pavel added.

"If you can call fifteen years a newcomer," Rotham pointed out. "Louise was telling me this morning that she was in London for ten years before coming here. Are you all finished delivering the invitations?"

"Yes, we are just about to get the gig," Pavel replied. "Unless you would like to take us home in your curricle?" he added hopefully.

"Where did you plan to sit, on the horse's back? You know the sporting rig only seats two. You can drive the gig home, Pavel. I shall drive Sissie." He made this announcement with very much the air of conferring a favor on the lady.

Miranda felt the temptation strongly enough, but

43

she disliked his arrogance at assuming she would jump at the chance.

"I shall go home in the gig, as I came," she said grandly.

"So there!" Rotham added, biting back a smile at her little show of independence. He liked a filly with spirit.

"That is dashed sporting of you, Sissie," Pavel said. "I shall go with Rotham. Can I take the ribbons?"

"And they say chivalry is dead," Rotham said. "But of course you may take the ribbons—of the gig. We cannot have Sissie driving home alone."

"I can handle Dobbin perfectly well!" she assured him.

"I have no doubt of it, but can you handle the derision of your friends, who will think you no better than a hoyden?"

It occurred to her that Rotham must consider her a young lady now, as he was worried about her reputation. "Yes, better than I could handle their derision at seeing me driving with you, I expect," she replied thoughtlessly.

Rotham chose to take it as a joke. It was either that or demand an explanation, or an apology, or some damned thing. But he felt the sting of her insult.

"Perhaps you had best come with me, Pavel," she said.

"You could beg a drive back with Louise. She is at Lafleur's," Pavel suggested.

"And let Dobbin find his own way home?" she asked.

The three went together back to the Mermaid.

"Surely you did not bring Castlereagh's brandy in your curricle?" Pavel mentioned.

"Brandy?" Rotham asked. "Oh, the brandy—no, Macpherson will deliver it to Ashmead," he said, but he looked slightly disconcerted.

Miranda took the idea his trip to Hythe had nothing to do with brandy. He had gone there on some other business, possibly something to do with the black trunk—or possibly to find a worthy recipient for the rose silk.

At the Mermaid, Rotham saw them off. "Tell Mama I shall be home for lunch. I am just stopping at the taproom for an ale before I leave."

They were not taken in by this trickery. They drove around the corner and waited. They had not long to wait. Within a minute—not nearly long enough to order and consume an ale—he was darting off in his curricle. He drove, and was followed by them, to Madame Lafleur's little cottage, which had roses clambering over the front.

"Another waste of time," Pavel said. "He is going to give Louise a drive home in the curricle. Laurent's nose will be out of joint."

It was not Louise that had taken Rotham haring off, however. He had spotted Monsieur Berthier's rig passing the inn and was curious enough to follow him. Berthier had expressed some reservations about returning a certain purloined item to France. He was not averse to doing it, but was concerned how it should be accomplished. He would "have a word with friends," he said, and let Rotham know that night at the rout. Rotham had not thought Madame Lafleur had any contact with France, after having been away from her homeland for so long. He had assumed Berthier's "friends" were the Gentlemen of the smuggling community.

He waited for fifteen minutes, driving around town and making frequent passes at the corner that gave a view of Madame Lafleur's residence. Should he join them? No, best not. He saw Louise's carriage outside and assumed she was asking Madame Lafleur to chaperon her in Brighton. He had told Berthier the matter was top secret, so he would say nothing in front of the Valdors. He drove home, followed at a discreet distance by the whisky.

"Why did he not go into Madame Lafleur's?" Pavel kept asking. "His presence would have insured her chaperonage. He kept driving around, looking at the house."

"Who was the other man? Perhaps that was who he was following."

"That was Berthier, who he mentioned last night might accompany Louise to Vienna," Pavel replied.

"What does he do?"

"Nothing; he is a gentleman. He has an estate over Hythe way."

"Hythe! That is where Rotham was going. I wonder if he called on Berthier."

"And Berthier went darting straight off to Lafleur's, another Frenchie. By Jove, I think we are on to something here, Sissie."

"Yes, but what?"

"I've no idea," he admitted, but still it was interesting, and surely significant.

Chapter Five

With a rout party to prepare for, Miranda could not spend her whole day spying. She had to send home for the blue peau de soie evening gown Trudie had given her. Miranda had planned the gown's debut at the local assembly in two weeks time, thus had not yet hemmed it. As the hemming would mean an hour in the privacy of her room, she decided to apply a strawberry mask to bleach the sprinkling of freckles that were summer's special gift to her. She worked by the window, where she could keep an eye on the bluejay. It was now harassing a sparrow.

Pavel returned to Rye to stroll cunningly up and down the street in front of Madame Lafleur's doorway. He did not see Berthier for the very good reason that Monsieur Berthier was at Ashmead.

This important discovery was not made until the family and their guests assembled for dinner. Louise took the shine out of even the fashionable gown Trudie had passed on to Miranda. Louise wore blue as well, a deep peacock blue gown of lustrine that shimmered and rustled enticingly when she moved. The Valdor diamonds went exceedingly well with it, and with the satin white bosom on which they rested.

47

Mr. Berthier could hardly take his eyes off her. This was of no concern to Miranda. She took little interest in a gentleman old enough to be her papa. Berthier was considered quite a catch by the older ladies and widows, who had no objection to a distinguished touch of silver at the temples. He was of medium height and well formed, with a dashing pair of brown eyes. Laurent fidgeted when Berthier claimed a seat by Louise and flirted outrageously with her. Rotham, sitting beside Miranda while awaiting the dinner announcement, watched the show with tolerant amusement.

"I see you have invited Mr. Berthier to the rout, Rotham," she said, hoping to do a little discreet quizzing about him.

"I observe you avoid the word *our* by calling it *the* rout. What have you against joint ownership with me? After all, it is only a rout, not a house, or a child."

"How silly you are," she said with a matronly *tsk*. "Berthier was not on *our* list. There—does that satisfy you?"

"Not entirely. The list was yours and Pavel's. It is the rout of which we have joint custody."

"Is he a particular friend of yours—Berthier I mean?"

"No, he is an admirer of Louise's," he replied. Then he inclined his head close to hers and added in a flirtatious tone, "As he is too old for you, I felt he would provide me no serious competition this evening." He waited—in vain—for the expected blush of pleasure, the shy smile.

"You invited him this morning while you were at Hythe arranging for Castlereagh's brandy?" she asked.

"Yes, I happened to bump into him on the High Street. A spare bachelor is always welcome at a do such as this."

"Is he one of those Huguenots you spoke of this morning?"

"No, he came to England much later."

"Like Madame Lafleur," she said pensively.

Madame Lafleur had also been invited to dinner. Miranda turned to study her. She was not as young as Louise, but by no means too old for Berthier. She would never see thirty again, but Miranda doubted she had yet seen forty. The French ladies aged well. Her coppery hair was stylishly arranged, and her figure was not too full to be admired.

Rotham said, "Just so," and spoke of other things. "The Breckenbridge brothers and their sister have agreed to supply music this evening. Miss Breckenbridge is quite an adept at the pianoforte."

"Yes, she plays at all the small parties."

"I hope you will save me a dance. The second dance, that is. Duty before pleasure," he said, gazing into her eyes.

Miranda failed to perceive, or at least respond to, the compliment lurking there. "Will you be leaving for London tomorrow morning?"

"Why is my departure of such interest to you, Sissie?"

"You are not likely to have a second party, and you do have urgent business in London, do you not?"

"Indeed I have, after I have finished my urgent business here."

He saw the leap of interest in her eyes. "What business is that, Rotham?" she asked, with a very poor simulation of nonchalance.

"Why, entertaining you, to be sure, *ma petite*," he said, patting her fingers in an avuncular way. A smile twitched his lips when she jerked her hand away. He watched as a scowl seized her face. "What have I said? Why do you mistake my poor efforts at friendship for an insult? You refuse to drive in my curricle—"

"Friendship? You do not know the meaning of the word. And if you think I am entertained by being pawed in public—" It was his secrecy about the black trunk that annoyed her, but she did not want to quiz him about it directly.

"You are quite right," he said. Then added, "We shall wait until we have privacy before we continue with the pawing."

He was saved from further aggravation by the butler's announcement of dinner. A formal dinner at Ashmead was a matter of some concern to Miranda. She was intimidated by the vast array of silver and the three wineglasses by her plate. There would be much too much food, all of it more elaborately prepared than her mama served at Wildwood. With Pavel by her side, however, she knew help was at hand if she ran amok with the cutlery. She was relieved, yet in some way also disappointed, when Rotham was seated at the other side of the table.

Her dinner partners were Pavel and Mr. Berthier. She did not need Pavel's commanding wink to urge her to quiz Berthier, but Berthier, like Rotham, proved a perfect oyster. Over the soup they spoke of what was on everyone's mind, Bonaparte's escape and its possible consequences. It was over the turbot in white sauce that Berthier admitted, after a few prods, that he had come to England at the time of the French Revolution.

"To escape the guillotine?" she asked artfully. Louise had said categorically he was not an aristo, so if he lied . . . Well, it might be some sort of clue.

"Nothing so melodramatic. My family was not noble. While on holiday in England a year before, I had met an *Anglaise* whom I hoped to marry. Unfortunately, the lady had the good sense to refuse me. With matters so unsettled in my homeland, I bought a farm in England and found it suited me very well. My mama was English," he said. "Her bachelor brother died and left me a small competence."

After the gentlemen had taken their port, they rejoined the ladies in the Blue Saloon. Other guests arrived, and a group went to the ballroom for some dancing. Madame Lafleur and Berthier tagged along, to stake their claim to the last remnants of youth. When Rotham led Louise to the floor for the minuet, Laurent walked stiffly to Miranda and asked her to stand up with him. He led her to Rotham's set and never took his eyes off Louise. Conversation was impossible; Miranda felt it was all he could do to follow the steps of the dance.

When the first set was over, Rotham came to her. "Our duty is done," he said, smiling, "and now we can have our dance."

"Thank goodness," she replied, with such passion that Rotham blinked in surprise.

"Why, I am flattered, Sissie. I did not realize you were looking forward to it as eagerly as I."

"I was looking forward to being rid of Laurent,"

she said. "If he is so mad for Louise, why does he not offer for her? I felt I was dancing alone."

"He don't offer for her because he cannot afford to keep her. Louise is expensive. His only chance in that quarter is if he reclaims the Valdor estate. He is the heir now. He will be the Comte de Valdor, not just Comte Laurent. A different matter altogether."

Like the difference between Lord Pavel and Lord Rotham, she thought. Rotham was quite alive to his eligibility. "Do you think he will ever recover his estate?"

"What you are asking is whether I think Boney will make good his attempt to regain control. I am tempted to say, 'I hope so,' but as a loyal Englishman, I must insist he has not a chance in the world. And now, as a renowned flirt, I shall bethump you with no more politics. We can find more interesting things to discuss—like your gown. Very fetching, Sissie. Is it also a gift from Trudie? Its being blue, and a fair match for his beloved's eyes, suggests that Parnham would be loath to part with it."

"She did not like the cut. Rotham, what did you mean, you are tempted to hope so?" she demanded.

"What, no pinpricks regarding my vile treatment of Trudie? It is unlike you to ignore such an opportunity."

"Oh, do talk sense," she said impatiently.

"Well, I shall try, but I can promise little. Common sense is not my long suit. I spoke without thinking. You have no idea how much trouble that habit has got me into. Naturally I did not mean I hope Bonaparte wins the war, only that I was tempted. I do not always fall victim to my tempta-

52

tions, whatever you might have heard from a lady who shall remain nameless."

"But why were you tempted to even *hope* Boney wins?"

"Being a perfect pattern card of selfishness, I was thinking of myself. It would be fine to be a hero."

"How could you be a hero if Bonaparte wins? You are not French."

He did not answer for a moment. He just gave an enigmatic smile, then said, "Strange things happen, Sissie. A man can be a small-scale hero without winning a war. Nothing in the line of a Wellington or a Bonaparte, but only a footnote in some tedious history book. It is really quite deflating to consider one's insignificance in the grand scheme of things."

"You can console yourself that you are cock of the walk here in the parish."

Miranda made a few attempts to make him explain that historical footnote, but had no success. At the end of the set, Rotham excused himself. The dance had not gone as he had anticipated. He was not one inch closer to teaching Sissie a lesson. In fact, he had the lowering impression that she was teaching him one. Flattery, gifts, insincerity, and flirtation did not work with her. What would it take to catch her interest?

Pavel beckoned to Miranda, and she went to him.

"Now is as good a time as any," he said. "Are you ready to let out a holler? When you see the Blue Lady, I mean?"

"Where is Rotham? We do not want him to land in on us."

"There is to be a short intermission. I believe he took Louise to the refreshment parlor. Laurent was looking daggers at him and latched on to Lafleur to pretend he was not jealous as a green cow. I have the ladder all ready. Let us go. I shall leave by the library door."

As soon as Pavel left, Miranda nipped out of the ballroom and up the curved staircase. The upper hallway was dimly lit with a lamp at either end. At the far end there hung a tapestry so old and dim the scene was nearly illegible. It was called *The Armada* and presumably showed the sinking of the Spanish Armada. She hastened along the corridor, past closed doors to the west end, just outside Rotham's bedroom. Both his door and Slack's were closed. She took a breath to steady the quaking inside and shrieked as loud as she could. A piercing scream rent the air.

"The Blue Lady! Help! She will kill me!" Then she sank to the floor in a graceful heap, with Trudie's blue peau de soie artfully arranged around her legs. She had no sooner closed her eyes than Rotham's door burst open. She kept her eyes tightly closed, but she felt a man's strong arms encircle her waist, lifting her head and shoulders from the floor. It did not feel like Slack; she had an impression of a bigger man.

"Good God! She has fainted." It was Rotham's voice! And he sounded genuinely concerned. "Get some brandy, Louise."

Louise was with him! They had been in his bedchamber together. Her eyes flew wide open, but fortunately Rotham did not see them. He was cradling her in his arms, gently crooning, with her head on his shoulder. She had not thought Rotham capable of such tenderness.

"There, there, my dear," he said comfortingly. "It

54

is all right. I am here. You are safe. There is no ghost."

Louise ran back into Rotham's room and came running with a bottle of brandy.

"I had best put her on my bed," Rotham said.

So saying, he lifted Miranda bodily from the floor and carried her into his room. A new sensation washed through her as he carried her in his arms. She felt vulnerable, with her feet off the ground, yet safe, even cherished. She wanted to put her arms around his neck, but caught herself in time. She let her arms dangle loosely in a very good simulation of unconsciousness. She felt herself being laid tenderly on his counterpane. She peered through her lashes as his hand brushed her cheek and saw Rotham gazing softly down at her.

Rotham was also aware of new emotions. Her skin was as soft and dewy as a rose petal. Long lashes fanned her youthful cheeks. She looked as innocent as a child. He would stop teasing her and leave her in her innocence.

Miranda felt a slight breeze and saw the open window just at the end of the bed, so she did not have to turn her head to see when Pavel arrived. She hoped he would not rush in before she got Rotham to take her to her room. Louise's presence made everything more difficult.

As she gazed the outline of a head appeared briefly at the window. Between the darkness and the filtered view seen through her eyelashes, she could not actually recognize Pavel, but of course it was he. She lay tense, willing him not to come barging in. He took one look at the scene in the room, and his head disappeared.

A moment's confusion ensued. Louise gasped and

pulled at Rotham's arm. "There was someone at the window, Rotham!" she exclaimed.

Rotham gave a start of surprise. He was going to rush to the window and catch Pavel. How could she stop him? She rose like Lazarus from the pillow, opened her eyes, threw herself into his arms, and said, "Oh, please, don't leave me! I am so frightened."

She felt the tension in his arms, the eagerness to push her aside and dart to the window. She clung to him like a barnacle. "Just for a moment, my dear," he said, trying to ease out of her arms.

She held on for all she was worth, trying desperately to think of some other ruse to give Pavel time to remove the ladder. She trembled with agitation and pressed her head into the nook between his shoulder and neck. "I had a horrid nightmare, Papa!" she said in a small, quavering voice. She did not know where the "Papa" came from, unless it was an instinctive wish to let Rotham know it was not him she was throwing herself at.

His arms tightened around her. The first thrill of her words, the soft, warm pressure of her body thrusting against his started an instinctive response. But when he heard that trusting, childlike "Papa," the seed of desire was transformed to a more gentle, protective feeling.

He cradled her a moment in his arms. "It is all right, Sissie. There is no cause for fear." Over her shoulder he said to Louise, "Call Slack to check the window. He is in my sitting room."

Louise ran to the sitting room and called to Slack.

Rotham reluctantly laid Miranda back on the pillow as Slack came running in. He brushed a tousle of curls from her forehead. Miranda assumed Pavel had had time to get down the ladder and whisk it out of sight.

"What happened? Is it safe?" Slack demanded.

Rotham's voice was quelling. "Take a look out the window, Slack. The comtesse thought she saw someone."

Slack ran to the window, raised it another foot, stuck his head out, and looked all around, then pulled his head back in. "All is clear," he said, staring in confusion at Miranda.

"Miss Vale fainted in the hallway," Rotham explained.

Miranda saw Slack's eyes slide to the corner of the room. "I see. Can I help?" he asked.

"We can handle it," Rotham replied.

"I'll leave you to it, then," Slack said, and returned to the sitting room.

Miranda turned her gaze to the spot where Slack had been looking. In the corner on a chair sat the battered black trunk. It was closed, but it was not locked. How could she get rid of everyone for a moment, to see what was in the trunk?

"How are you feeling?" Rotham asked her. "Where is that brandy, Louise?" he called over his shoulder.

Louise poured a little brandy into a glass and handed it to him. He lifted Miranda's head from the pillow and held the glass to her lips. "Take a sip, my dear. It will do you good."

She took a sip and nearly choked. It felt like ice, yet it burned like fire, and tasted horrid. Her body refused to accept such poison. She could feel her throat reject it and put her hands to her mouth to prevent staining Trudie's blue peau do soie with brandy.

Rotham pressed a handkerchief into her fingers. She looked at him, her eyes watering from the strong drink.

"Shall I call Lady Hersham?" Louise asked.

"There is no need to disturb Mama," Rotham replied. "But perhaps you could go belowstairs and explain if anyone asks for Sissie," he added.

Miranda was relieved when Louise left. Now if only she could get rid of Rotham for a moment.

He proffered the brandy again. "Another sip. It will revive you," he said. She let him hold it to her lips, but she did not drink. Her mind was busy, trying to invent a ruse to get him out of the room.

"You are not drinking, Sissie," he said, and raised the glass higher, until the brandy was right in her nostrils.

She pushed the hand holding the glass away rather forcefully, splashing the drink. The spill landed on his handkerchief.

"I am all right, Rotham," she said angrily.

"Ah good, you know who I am. I feared you had addled your brain when you mistook me for your papa. What happened? Why were you screaming in the hallway?"

Miranda found she could not look him in the eye. She felt the heat of embarrassment flush her cheeks and began fiddling with the counterpane. "It was the Blue Lady," she said.

Rotham began to smell a rat. He cupped her chin in his fingers and tilted her head up, forcing her to meet his gaze. She lowered her long lashes. "And now the truth, miss."

"It is true! I saw her, just at the top of the kitchen stairs."

"What were you doing there? Your room is at the

other end of the hallway. Mama never puts young ladies at this end of the house."

She gave him an angry look. "I wonder why? It was not at all the thing for you to have Louise in your bedroom with the door closed."

"You cannot think— Good God, what do you take me for?"

"A rake, milord. I should think you could behave yourself under your papa's roof, and with your cousin at that."

A clever minx. Were ladies born knowing that offense was the best defense? Here he had been taking—mistaking—her for an innocent child. The angry gray eyes staring at him were the eyes of a woman. "It is difficult, when ladies will insist on throwing themselves into my arms."

She knew it was not the comtesse they were discussing now. His sharp eyes told her so. "I did not throw myself in your arms. I fainted. And don't try to tell me Louise fainted, too, for she was wide awake."

Rotham gritted his teeth in an effort to hold in the profanity that rose to his throat. How dare the chit call him to account, as if she were his mama. "Not that it is your concern, but it happens Louise and I were discussing business," he said.

"I do not have to inquire what sort of business."

"And I do not have to listen to this impertinence from a schoolgirl. It is your lascivious mind that colors an innocent meeting in these lurid hues. You are certainly Trudie Vale's sister! No one can match a prude for salacious imaginings."

"I am not a prude!"

"Then don't talk like one. You did not answer my

question. What were you doing loitering outside my door?"

"I was not loitering! I was passing by."

"It is not necessary to pass my doorway to get to your chamber from the front staircase."

An instant's reflection told her this was true. "I came up the servants' staircase," she lied.

"Oh." This quite took the wind out of Rotham's sails. He did not question that she had been in the kitchen. Sissie had been visiting Pavel since she was in short skirts. They were as likely to be in the kitchen as anywhere else. Once this was settled, he was seized by another question. "What did you see outside my door?"

"I saw the Blue Lady—just a fleeting glance."

"You know perfectly well there is no such thing as ghosts. What you saw was a real live person, probably a lady in blue," he said, frowning. "Think, Sissie. Can you remember anything about her? Might it have been a man wearing a domino or some such thing?"

This surprising suggestion threw her into a quandary. "I only had a glimpse," she said uncertainly.

"Was she listening at the keyhole?"

"No, she was just—floating at the top of the stairs."

"Did she wear a hat? What color was her hair?"

"She was all blue," Miranda said in confusion. It was beginning to dawn on her that Rotham believed a real live person had been spying outside his doorway. "It was not Laurent, following you and Louise, if that is what you think. He was still in the ballroom when I left."

"Was he, by God? That is interesting."

Miranda sat a moment, trying to think whether she should just ask him point-blank what was going on. Before she made up her mind, there was a pounding on the servants' stairs and Pavel came pouncing into the room.

"Rotham! Sissie—what the deuce is going on? I was looking all over for you, Sissie."

Rotham gave him a searching look. "Strange you should come looking for Sissie in my bedchamber."

"Yes, and it is strange that I found her here, too," Pavel riposted.

"I saw the Blue Lady, and I fainted," Miranda said to Pavel, with a commanding look. "I believe if you will both just leave me alone a moment to recuperate, I shall be well enough to go back downstairs soon."

"I shall take you to your own room," Rotham said. His eyes just flickered to the corner where the trunk stood unlocked.

"Oh, I could not walk yet. I must rest a little."

"I shall carry you," he said firmly.

Miranda thought their plan had failed, but at that moment, Rotham said, "I shall just have a word with Slack before we go," and left the room, closing the door behind him.

"The trunk is in the corner. Come quickly," Miranda said, leaping up from the bed.

She and Pavel darted to the trunk and lifted the lid. They saw a piece of old linen, faded to brown. It looked antique. It was embroidered in various colors with a series of pictures. There was a king and a castle and courtiers. Pavel lifted the end, and they saw more men, a whole fleet of boats with oddly shaped sails, and a tree.

The thing was too large to examine properly. It

was about twenty inches wide and very long, maybe hundreds of feet. Pavel unfolded it, and she saw groups of men with spears and swords, some of them mounted. The men wore small pointed caps. Their clothing was embroidered in strange little circles, perhaps to simulate metal armor. There were words embroidered across the top. She thought they might be Latin, or at least not English or French. She tried to read the printing. Some of the words were names—Eadward, Willelm, Harold. Strange mythical beasts were embroidered in a border along the top and bottom.

"Best close the trunk before he comes back," Miranda said.

They closed the lid, and she rushed back to Rotham's bed, just as the door to Slack's room opened and Rotham returned.

"I shall take you to your room now," he said. Before she had time to object, he scooped her off the bed, into his arms as easily as if she were a rag doll.

There was no recurrence of that cherished feeling the first time he had swept her off her feet. Rotham's face, only inches from hers, wore an angry expression. At this close range, she could distinguish individual hairs of his eyebrows and long lashes. A faint spicy scent clung about him. She had not thought Rotham would use a man's scent. The arms holding her were powerful, but they were not gentle.

"I can walk," she announced, and began pushing at his arms.

He tossed her unceremoniously onto the bed, so hard that she bounced a few times before coming to rest. Rotham's scowl did not encourage her to chastise him, but she glared and drew herself up from the bed with what she hoped was dignity.

"Can I give you a hand?" Pavel offered, placing his arm around her waist to lead her out of the room.

"Thank you, Pavel," she said demurely, and with a sniff over her shoulder, they left.

Rotham closed the door and turned to glance at the trunk. It did not appear to have been disturbed. A frown creased his brow, and on an impulse, he quietly opened his door a crack. Sissie and Pavel did not go to Miranda's room but went downstairs. The young lady had made a miraculous recovery. She no longer required Pavel's assistance to negotiate her steps. She was walking perfectly well and chattering excitedly. He closed the door.

Had it all been an act, then? Had she been aware of what she was doing when she threw herself into his arms? He was demmed sure she had not seen a ghost—but what had she seen?

Slack's head appeared at the other door. "Is the comtesse going to do it?" he asked.

"No, I have decided against asking her to," Rotham replied.

"Did you show it to her?"

"No, I did not tell her I have it. I shall use a man for the job after all. It is too risky for a lady. I am going belowstairs, Slack. Lock the door behind me."

Chapter Six

"We must talk," Pavel said, leading Miranda into the library. This was one room that had no tapestries, due to the walls of books. A pair of lamps, one at either end of a long table, did but an indifferent job of lighting the chamber. The marble busts along the top shelves took on the eerie air of listeners. He lowered his voice. "That faded old piece of linen cannot be what all the fuss is about—Rotham locking his door and setting Slack to guard it."

"There was nothing else in the trunk—was there?" she asked. "I daresay there could have been a letter hidden beneath it, with the old embroidery a mere subterfuge."

"I never thought of that," he admitted. "I thought there might have been a secret message in the embroidery. There was printing all along the top."

"It looked as if it were hundreds of years old."

"A clever ruse," Pavel said. "They got hold of faded old material and embroidered a message in code on the cloth. Rotham is carrying a secret message to London; that is why he is keeping so close about his doings."

"Why does he not get on to London then?" she

asked. "He could have gone yesterday, instead of arranging a rout party."

"Pleasure before business—that is his motto. Said so himself. Mind you, he did send a footman off with a letter last night. He must be awaiting a reply. Pretty dangerous, hauling that message to London. Daresay he asked Castlereagh to send a code breaker here to read it. Much the safest way."

"Rotham arrived yesterday afternoon. The message could have been in London last night. If it were urgent, the code breaker would have been here before now."

"P'raps he is," Pavel said, with a sapient look. "P'raps Rotham sent a message off on the sly before he came home."

"You mean Berthier? Rotham went to visit him in Hythe this morning."

"Aye, and he is here now, staying a few days, by the by. He will dope out the message tonight and hotfoot it off to London tomorrow."

"He is taking his time about it. And what was Louise doing in Rotham's room? He said it was business."

"Nothing to do with this business," Pavel scoffed. "They would be arranging their tryst in Brighton. Rotham would not take her to bed under Papa's roof."

"I think you are quite mistaken about the embroidery," she said. "Rotham said he half hoped Boney wins, and he—Rotham—would be a hero. I think he is a turncoat."

Pavel blustered up at this. "No such a thing! Damme, he wanted to join the army, but Papa would not let him."

"Berthier is a Frenchman, after all, and Rotham

went running straight to him this morning. Castlereagh would not use Berthier to decode secret messages. He would have specially trained men in London."

"Then Berthier is not decoding the message. He is only here for the party. Rotham would never turn his coat."

"He said Bonaparte is the greatest man of the age."

"The greatest Frenchman, even if he is a Corsican. Everyone knows Wellington is the greatest man of our generation." He sat, frowning into the grate. "Though it is odd Wellington sent Rotham packing," he said, chewing at his thumbnail. "You don't suppose he did it to get rid of Rotham?"

Miranda knew she ought to encourage this notion. It was she who had suggested that Rotham was a turncoat. She found, to her dismay, that what she really wanted was for Pavel to convince her she was mistaken.

"Wellington must trust him if he sent him home with this special message," she said uncertainly.

"But did he send him? You remember what we heard outside the study door. Papa gave him a rare Bear Garden jaw. Called him mad, said he had brought disgrace on the family name. A hanging matter. That sounds like treason. Said he must take it back at once. I believe Rotham has shabbed off with some secret document. In fact, Rotham told Papa in so many words that Castlereagh didn't know he had it. Papa told him to write to Castlereagh at once. I doubt the letter was ever written."

"If he did steal a secret message, it was all her doing—Louise's," Miranda said angrily. "The embroidered piece must be what all the fuss is about. I recall your papa saying Lady Hersham must see it. It was the embroidery they showed her, for she said it was ugly, and she had better work at home."

"Which she has. So, what is to do?"

"We must steal it to prevent Rotham from delivering it to—to whoever he plans to deliver it to."

"We cannot get into his room. What we'll do, we'll keep a sharp eye on the old cloth and seize it from the French spy after Rotham has turned it over."

"Who could his accomplice be?" Miranda asked.

"Some French spy here in England. Could be Berthier."

"Rotham did go running off to see him, and now Berthier is here."

"Looks demmed suspicious," Pavel agreed. "A fine shot, Berthier. He killed a man in a duel a dozen or so years ago. Something to do with a lady, I believe."

"Well, if you are afraid of Berthier—"

"I did not say I was afraid of him!"

"But you are, so the only other recourse open to us is to steal the embroidery. In that way, Rotham cannot give it to the French spies. We must get back into his room."

Pavel considered it a moment and found no fault in this scheme. "Demmed clever thinking, Sissie. Now, how shall we set about it? We will have to wait until the dead of night, when Rotham and Slack are asleep."

"Is there another key for Rotham's room?" she asked.

"Papa has a full set in his study. I shall sneak number seventeen off the ring now, while Papa is busy at the card table."

They hastened out of the library and into Lord Hersham's study. By the light from the hallway, Pavel found the tinderbox and lit a lamp. A large, square room done in paneled oak sprang into dim view. The dark oak soaked up the light, turning the corners into shadows, but it was only the oak desk that interested them. Pavel opened the middle drawer and lifted a heavy ring holding three dozen keys. He began squinting at the numbers stamped on the keys. The keys clinked and rattled as he worked through them, once quickly, then again, more slowly.

He looked up and said, "Number seventeen is missing. I daresay Rotham took it, along with the spare key from Cook's ring. Damme, now how are we to steal the embroidery?"

They were about to extinguish the lamp and leave when a shadow loomed up at the doorway. Pavel fully expected it would be Papa, catching him red-handed. He hastily prepared an excuse for having the keys.

"Ah, Papa! I was just going to borrow the key— *Rotham!*"

Lord Rotham stepped in and closed the door quietly behind him. "Which key was that, Pavel?" he asked. His menacing smile looked more deadly than a charged pistol.

Pavel's mouth opened, but no words came out.

Miranda gave a nervous laugh. "We are caught dead to rights, Pavel," she said. "We were going to steal a bottle of—of your papa's best Burgundy from the cellar."

Rotham shook his head. "You will have to do better than that, children. You know perfectly well Cook has keys to the wine cellar. She would not object to getting you a bottle of Burgundy. In fact, you will find some bottles on the sideboard in the dining room. You should have said champagne."

He reached out and lifted the keys from Pavel's fingers. He examined them hastily, much as Pavel had done. When he discovered number seventeen was missing, his face stiffened to stone.

Miranda had the strange sensation she could read the working of the mind behind the mask. He did not know the key was missing. He did not have it, as she had thought. Who had it?

Rotham's hand went out. He tossed the keys in the drawer and closed it, then held his open palm out to Pavel. "I am afraid I must ask you for the key to my room, Pavel," he said.

"But we don't have it! I admit we was looking for it, but it ain't here."

Rotham looked from Pavel to Miranda. "It is true," she said. "We did come looking for it, but it is gone."

Their faces were an open book. They were telling the truth. "Ask Papa if he has it, Pavel."

Pavel was happy to escape.

"Why did you want the key to my room?" he asked Miranda.

She decided it was time to bring the whole matter into the open. "To prevent you from betraying England," she said nobly. "We know about the black trunk, and the embroidery, Rotham. You must not do it."

He stood still as a statue, looking and listening and thinking. "You saw the embroidery? That is why you 'fainted' outside my room, for an excuse to get inside and snoop?"

"Yes, we did not know you were there."

"Then you did not really see anyone listening at my door?"

"No, we pretended I had seen the Blue Lady. Who did you think was listening?"

"I don't know." He leveled a dark stare at her. "It seems I can trust no one. How did you know I had—something of interest in my room?"

"Everyone knows it by now. It was the black trunk. Pavel said you did not take it with you. And when you were giving Louise the green silk, Laurent mentioned that the silks were not in the black trunk, that you had had the black trunk taken to your room as soon as you arrived."

A light of interest flashed in his eyes. "Laurent said that?" he asked.

"Something of the sort, yes." After a moment, she asked, "Is it Laurent you are afraid of?"

"Afraid?" His eyebrows climbed up toward his hairline. "I have nothing to fear from Laurent."

"We—Pavel and I—thought there might be a secret message in the words of the embroidery. If there is something of the sort, Rotham, you must take it to Castlereagh at once. Whatever price the French promised you, you cannot betray your own country."

He blinked in bewilderment, then as realization dawned, his face clenched to anger. His words, when he spoke, came out in a bark. "What the devil are you talking about? Do you take me for a traitor?"

"Your own papa spoke of it being a hanging matter!"

"So you heard that as well. You don't miss much. I begin to think it is you and Pavel who should be helping me."

A smile trembled on her lips. "Then you are not selling information to Berthier?" she asked.

"So it is Berthier you have chosen as my accomplice in treason, is it?"

"It would not be treason for him. He is French."

Rotham ran his fingers distractedly through his hair. "It is not what you think, Sissie. I am not engaged in any treasonous business," he said, with what looked like sincerity. "It is something else entirely. I acted with the best of intentions, but foolishly. Very foolishly," he said with a sad sigh. "I am merely trying to undo the harm I might have done."

"What did you do?"

"I took something that did not belong to me. Not money or secret messages, nothing of that sort. It was a—a sort of symbolic gesture, done from misguided patriotism when I was too foxed to think straight."

"Is that true, Rotham?"

He met her look with a steady gaze. "As God is my witness." Then his expression softened to a smile. "And I did not smuggle Louise up to my chamber to make love to her either."

He continued gazing at her until she felt a weakness invade her. Why was he looking at her like that, as if it actually mattered to him what she thought? As if he cared for her good opinion above everything.

"Pavel said you would not do so, under your papa's roof," she said primly.

His nostrils pinched. "Kind of Pavel. I must remember to thank him for that edifying reading of my character. Naturally I do all my seducing away from home. We dumb animals do not usually foul our own nests."

"No one called you a dumb animal. Quite the contrary; you are sly, Rotham. Why will you not tell us what you are doing?"

"I have told you."

"You only spoke of a symbolic gesture."

"I have no doubt you will discover it for yourself ere long. You seem to have ferreted out all my other secrets."

He looked at the drawer holding the keys. If Papa did not have the key . . .

The sound of flying feet alerted them to Pavel's return. He came in, gasping for breath and nearly falling when he tripped on the carpet edge. "Papa don't have it," he announced. "He says it has been on his ring all along, or ought to have been. He did not actually check, you know, but where else would it be? He keeps all the spare keys there."

"Someone has got hold of it!" Miranda exclaimed, with a frightened look at Rotham. Then she turned to Pavel, who was squinting at her in an effort to silence her. "He already knows we know about the embroidery," she said. "Do you remember, Pavel, when we were in the library discussing getting the spare key from Cook, we saw someone sneaking away." Pavel's expression turned to a murderous glare.

"What the deuce are you rattling on about, Sissie?"

"He knows," she repeated. "I told him everything."

"You omitted that bit, but I believe I understand," Rotham said. "You tried to get the key for my room from Cook. Someone overheard and realized there was another key in the house."

"Exactly," Miranda said, and rushed on to the more important matter. "Rotham is not a traitor after all, Pavel."

"I did not really think you was," Pavel said. "I figured you must have been bosky, or mixed up with a French woman. But what is going on, Rotham?"

Rotham felt a sharp stab of anger at Pavel's thoughtless words. Was this the opinion his young brother had of him? The anger softened to regret as he admitted this reading of his character was justified. He did drink too much, and he was no stranger to the muslin company, but it shamed him to have it all blurted out in front of Sissie Vale. Her opinion of him was bad enough without this.

"More to the point," he countered, "whom did you see sneaking away when you left the library?"

"We did not get a look at him, but it was a man," Pavel said. "It might even have been a footman. It was dark, you know, but I could see it was not a lady's skirt. It was trousers, or it could have been a footman's breeches. That was before Berthier arrived. It could have been Laurent."

"Yes, it could have been Laurent," Rotham agreed.

"About the old linen, Rotham," Pavel said. "Is it a secret message?"

"No, it is only a symbol," Miranda told him.

"Of what?" Pavel asked in confusion.

"Of France," Rotham said. "It is of the utmost importance that no one knows I have it. My plan is to return it if—depending on how events turn out in Europe."

"Depending on whether or not Boney wins?" Pavel asked.

"Yes."

"So that is why you ain't rushing it off to London? You are waiting to hear of Wellington's victory?"

"Exactly. Meanwhile, say nothing to anyone. We must guard the black trunk with our lives."

Both Miranda and Pavel felt a swell of excitement quiver through them. "We will do anything you say, Rotham," Miranda said, with glowing eyes.

"Anything? Now that is a delightful and unexpected bonus," he murmured in a way she could not trust.

"Anything to help you guard the black trunk," she explained.

"I knew there would be limits to your amiability. What we must do now is have a waltz."

"I do not see how that can help!" she objected.

"We must keep up an appearance of normalcy. Pavel will run upstairs, give five light knocks on my door, which will bring Slack to inquire for the password, '*C'est moi.*' You will tell Slack that Papa's key has been stolen and he must on no account leave the room for so much as an instant."

"*C'est moi,*" Pavel said, to make sure he had the words right.

"Just so."

"Right, I am off then. Carry on."

"That is just what we were about to do," Rotham said, placing Miranda's hand on his arm to lead her to the ballroom.

Chapter Seven

"What is that strange music the Brecken-bridges are playing?" Rotham asked, as they progressed toward the ballroom.

Miranda looked at him in astonishment. "Were they not dancing it at the Congress in Vienna, Rotham? It has been all the crack in London since the czar and King Frederick's visit. Fancy a smart like you not recognizing the waltz," she said, with a great air of superiority.

"Fancy anyone mistaking that racket for a waltz."

"Of course it is a waltz. We are not so backward as you think. We have been trying it since last winter."

"No doubt you will get it right, in another year or two. Someone ought to tell the fiddlers the waltz is played in three-quarter time."

"Why do you always have to find fault with everything?" she grumbled.

"Because, my little cabbage, I am an idealist. I like to think the world could be perfect, if only we all gave it our best effort."

He gathered her into his arms for the waltz. She held herself stiffly, determined not to fall under his sway. Miranda admitted to herself that Rotham was attractive, and of course, he was the premier catch in the neighborhood. That conferred an aura of glamour on him. A girl felt special when she was with Rotham. She could see all the other girls and their mamas looking at her with green-tinged eyes. She would be talked about tomorrow, her behavior scrutinized for signs of forwardness and Rotham's for tokens of susceptibility.

She said, "A pity you do not practice what you preach—about everyone being perfect, I mean."

A couple collided with them just as Rotham was attempting a turn. It was Madame Lafleur and a neighboring squire.

"A thousand pardons," she laughed gaily. "We are learners, milord. We have you to thank for bringing us up to date, *non?*"

The collision put them off their pace. When they recovered, Rotham said, "I believe you were hinting at a lack of perfection in me, Sissie. Was that a slur on my dancing? I cannot believe you are criticizing my jacket, for it is considered one of Weston's finest efforts. The czar himself complimented me on it."

She gave him a condescending look, though she was impressed with his boast. Imagine, she was dancing with a jacket admired by Czar Alexander! "How very superficial you are, Rotham. I was not talking about your dancing or your jacket but your manners. Trudie was right about you."

"It is my party after all. I am responsible for its imperfections."

"I thought it was ours," she reminded him.

"So it is, but I was disparaging myself for not doing better by my guests. How often are you going to throw Trudie in my face? I scarcely knew Trudie.

I stood up with her at a few country-dances. I called on her twice."

"Three times, counting the last time, when you jilted her. You only stayed two minutes."

Rotham was bumped from behind by an energetic couple. He trod on Miranda's toes and apologized brusquely. "I did not realize there was an optimum length for a jilting visit. I had matters to attend to in London." He was angered that this chit had the audacity to call him to account. What business was it of hers?

"The very serious business of flirting your way through the Season. You left in mid-April, just as the Season was beginning."

"Can we not discuss something other than Trudie?"

"We are not discussing Trudie. We are discussing your being so far from the ideal. The topic should be pleasing to you, as you are the center of it."

Now he was an egotist! He swallowed his ire and gave her his most killing smile. "There is nothing so enjoyable as being an object of criticism. Do you read the Bible, Sissie?"

"Of course."

"Then no doubt you are familiar with the precept, let him who is without sin cast the first stone. Have you never carried on an *à suivie* flirtation with any of the local bucks?"

"Of course I have, but I did not break their hearts."

He looked deeply into her eyes. "Are you quite certain of that? I wager those stormy seas of eyes have capsized a vessel or two."

Miranda felt a warm wash of pleasure surge through her. She had never thought of her eyes in terms of stormy seas or breaking men's hearts, though now that she considered her few flirtations, she admitted that Jeremy Faraday had been quite smitten. He had looked like a whipped pup when she'd dropped him.

"I did not do it on purpose at any rate," she protested.

"Ah, but when you are the possessor of such eyes, you must handle them with care. They carry an obligation, like wealth or power. You do the harm unwittingly. I felt my own hull beginning to quiver when you pitched yourself into my arms. In my bedroom—on my bed," he added, to lend it a wicked air.

"I called you papa, so you would not think I was—"

"Throwing yourself at me? It was a wise precaution, but very naughty of you all the same, to throw such powerful temptation in my way. I am only flesh and blood after all."

This was going too far. Miranda could not repress a gurgle of laughter. "I doubt you will flounder, Rotham. The whole country knows of your exploits. You have had greater temptation than me. I lay no claim to being a femme fatale. My only practice has been on locals. Your hulk must be made of stern stuff to have avoided rupture all these years."

"If that is a compliment, I thank you. I take leave to doubt the word 'hulk' was used in innocence, however. Hull is what I said. A nautical term—" He was required to dodge as a portly matron in puce and her red-faced partner bore down on him. "That was a close shave. We were nearly scuttled. I was about to point out that I am not Methuselah. 'All these years' has a nasty ring to it. You were in danger of igniting a fire, and a fire can burn down a castle as well as a barn."

"You are mixing your metaphors. We were discussing sinking ships."

"So we were, but one is usually consumed by the flames of love, not drowned in it."

"You sound like a cheap novel, Rotham."

"I see you are familiar with the genre."

The music came to a stop, and they walked off to the edge of the room.

"That was—interesting," Rotham said. "I thrive on danger. I wonder if we might take the Breckenbridges to London and start a new dance craze. Saint Vitus' Dance, we shall call it. Shall we have a glass of wine to aid our recovery from that steeplechase?"

"Very well."

With the jealous eyes of the local gentry on her, Miranda was not averse to walking off with Rotham, but she reminded herself she must not fall in love with him.

It was not until they were in the corridor en route to the refreshment parlor that she remembered the serious business going forth at Ashmead. It seemed incredible that she could have forgotten it.

"Should we not be doing something about discovering who has the key to your room?" she asked, rather reluctantly, for she was enjoying her brief flirtation with Rotham.

"You are right, of course. I am too easily distracted by a beautiful lady." His eyes gazed into hers, sending delightful shivers up her spine. "My besetting sin. Well, one of them at least. Let us go to the study and see if the key has been returned."

"It would not be put back yet. It has not been used."

"It will be a quiet place to think, and talk," he said, and led her down the corridor to Lord Hersham's oak-lined office. He looked in the desk drawer and examined the key ring.

"It is not here," he said. "The best way to learn who has it is to catch him—or her—red-handed. It was stolen for the purpose of getting into my room. Slack will be on guard."

As he spoke he poured two glasses of wine from the decanter on the desk and handed Miranda one.

"By her, I assume you mean the comtesse?" she asked, accepting the wine.

"That was my meaning, but now that you mention it, we must not forget Madame Lafleur is also here this evening. It would be interesting to get a peek in her reticule."

"Louise and Laurent called on her this morning," Miranda mentioned. "But, of course, you know that. You followed them."

A smile quirked his lips. "I have led you a merry chase, have I not?"

"We were in Rye to deliver the invitations anyway. You did not take us much out of our way. A pity Madame Lafleur is not younger, and you could have one of your flirtations with her—distract her while you rifled her reticule, I mean."

"You are inferring my flirtations have an ulterior motive. They don't. They are an end in themselves."

"I only meant you could put it to good use."

"I know what you meant. Getting a look in her reticule is not a bad idea."

"We should check Louise as well, but she is not

carrying an evening bag. She might have the key in a pocket, or hidden down her bodice," Miranda suggested. She had already chosen Louise as the culprit.

Rotham lowered his brow. "If you were about to suggest I have a flirtation with her to rifle her bosom, I pray you hold your tongue."

"I was not going to suggest that! Trudie never said—" A glare from his dark eyes stopped her. "You need not look so fierce, Rotham. You are a horrid flirt. I know you kissed Trudie behind the lime tree in the park. That is why she took the notion you were serious about her."

"You country girls get everything wrong—the waltz, a stolen kiss. Times are changing. A man does not marry every girl he steals a kiss from."

"A good thing, or you would be a bigam—triga—"

"Polygamist, I believe, is the word you are rooting about your poor little mind for. You make me sound like Bluebeard. It was only a little kiss."

"That is not what I heard," she replied, with a bold toss of her head.

"The well-known fury of a scorned woman, exaggerating her wrongs. She was not averse, I promise you. All I did was—this," he said, pulling her into his arms to try for a kiss.

The abrupt movement caught Miranda unawares. She suddenly found herself held tightly in Rotham's arms, with his dark head looming above hers. His handsome face wore a mischievous grin. It looked diabolical as his head lowered to hers. It was only a quick kiss, a sudden pressure against her lips, the intimate grazing of flesh on flesh, then he lifted his head, smiling, but he still held her tightly in his arms.

"There now, is that anything to get upset about?" he asked.

She tilted her head back and gazed into his eyes. Miranda had always thought his eyes were a deep, navy blue. At this close range, they looked like dark opals. There were specks of gold and silver shimmering in them. She wondered if it was a reflection from the lamp.

"No, certainly not," she said, and laughed nervously. "I had a better kiss than that from Pavel in the woodshed when I was six years old."

"Did you, by God? Then I cannot let the reputation of the philandering Hershams down. You are all grown up now, Sissie, and deserve a better cause for complaint."

His arms tightened, crushing her against his hard chest, as he lowered his head. Miranda felt a rising panic and wrenched her head aside as she tried to push him away. His arms held her like leather bands. While she struggled, he moved one arm and lifted her chin, twisting her face back to his.

He saw the glitter in her eyes and gazed into them, trying to determine whether it was fear or anger. He had no wish to frighten her. His first good intentions of not enjoying a flirtation with Sissie had died aborning when he learned of her ruse in his bedroom. She was not quite the innocent miss he had taken her for. As she had been playing off her tricks on him, he had no hesitation to reciprocate.

"Get your hands off me, you lecher!" she exclaimed.

Anger. It was definitely anger. That was all right, then. He held her chin up by main force and pressed his lips firmly on hers. It was his experience that an unwilling lady soon succumbed to masculine insistence. He gave it his best effort, moving his hands over her back in a reassuring way, while his lips made nibbling, encouraging motions against hers. The harder she tried to escape, the more he persisted. It became a test of his manhood, his desirability to women. Dammit, what was the matter with her? Was she frigid?

Miranda knew Rotham did not care for her. For him it was only a game. He was merely insisting on exercising his noble prerogative. The arrogance of it! Yet she was not entirely immune. There was some secret pleasure in his ardent insistence. She had never been kissed in this fashion before. It was strangely exciting. A tumultuous flutter in her breast warned of the danger in this game. When she remembered the month of Trudie's tears and recriminations, she feared she was heading down the same path and gave a final push that sent Rotham reeling back.

She tossed her head and glared. "You have finally succeeded in achieving perfection in one category, Rotham. What a perfectly rude, common, vulgar, repulsive creature you are. You ought to know better than to treat a young female guest in your papa's house so shabbily. Hersham would take you to the woodshed and give you a good thrashing if he knew what you were about."

Rotham just stared, trying to assimilate the flood of insults that poured over him. Repulsive, him? Bad enough he could not battle down her resistance, the final degradation was that she suggested Papa would thrash him, as if he were an unlicked cub. And to put the cap on it, she was right. He had behaved wretchedly.

"And you, madam, are a perfect shrew!"

"What did you expect, that I would sigh and moan like—"

He shook an imperious finger under her nose. "If I hear the name Trudie thrown in my face once more this evening, I shall—"

There was a discreet coughing sound from the doorway. It was the butler, standing with a perfectly impassive face. He had seen worse. "If you will pardon the interruption, your lordship, Lord Pavel has sent word down by a servant requesting your presence immediately abovestairs, in your lordship's chamber. A matter of the utmost importance, I understand."

Rotham and Miranda exchanged one horrified look. Rotham seized her hand and they took off, nearly capsizing the butler.

"Someone has got the black trunk!" Miranda exclaimed, as they darted upstairs.

"Impossible! Slack has a gun."

They turned right at the top of the stairs and pelted down the corridor. At the end they saw Pavel's head peering out the door, waiting for them.

"It is not gone!" Miranda gasped.

"No, it's still here," he replied. "It is Slack. I believe he's been poisoned."

Chapter Eight

They all went to Rotham's room and closed the door. When Miranda had been in the room before, she had been too busy fainting and acting to take much notice of it. It was a fine and lofty chamber, with heavy masculine furnishings and green velvet hangings on the canopied bed and windows.

"What kept you?" Pavel demanded querulously. "I sent word down to you ages ago. I could not leave the room unattended with the black trunk here, so I rang for a servant."

"We had left the ballroom," Miranda explained. "Boxer found us in your papa's office. We came up at once."

"Slack is in your sitting room, Rotham," Pavel continued. "I believe the poison was in the tea, or the food. He had been eating a snack. He was just as he is now when I arrived. The outer door was closed. I gave the five knocks and the password. When he did not answer, I tried the knob and walked right in."

Rotham opened the door, and they followed him into his sitting room, which Slack had been using as a bedroom during this period. Slack lay sprawled on the chaise longue on the other side of the room. On the sofa table before him lay the remains of a cold collation: mutton, bread, cheese, sweets, and a pot of tea.

"He ain't cold, but he has not moved since I got here," Pavel said, gazing fearfully at the inert body.

Rotham examined his valet, touching his cheek and feeling his pulse. "His pulse is sluggish. He has been given a sleeping powder." He poured some tea in the saucer and tasted it. "This is the culprit, I fancy."

"Should we call a doctor?" Miranda asked.

"Best to be sure, but I believe he is just sleeping soundly. Ask Boxer to call Makepiece, Pavel, and if the doctor would be so kind as to use the kitchen door. We do not want to disturb our guests."

"At least the embroidery is safe," Pavel said. "It is plain as a pikestaff that whoever stole Papa's key arranged for Slack to get the drugged drink. He obviously used the key—the door was unlocked—but he did not take the embroidery. He was after something else. What is it you ain't telling us, Rotham?"

Rotham did not immediately rush off to check any drawers or hunt for a different purloined item. "He was after the embroidery. Thank God he did not take it. Have a peek around the ballroom while you are belowstairs, Pavel, and see if anyone is missing."

"Who should I look for, in particular?"

Rotham rubbed his hand over his chin. "Madame Lafleur, Laurent, Berthier, and Louise as well. This was not the work of a neighbor, but someone who is staying here."

"I shall be back in two shakes of the lamb's tail," Pavel said, and scooted off.

"We could ask the servants who ordered the supper," Miranda suggested to Rotham.

"I shall speak to Cook when Pavel returns. You will not want to be left alone."

"I am not afraid! Slack is not dead after all but only sleeping. Go ahead, Rotham. We have not a minute to waste."

"There is no hurry. I need time to think," he said, and gestured to an upholstered chair. She sat in it; he sat at his desk. "Did you notice if Louise and Laurent were in the ballroom when we were waltzing?"

"Louise was there, dancing with Berthier, so he was there as well. You recall Madame Lafleur bumped into us."

"Yes, but I saw her leaving the room later."

"None of it proves anything. Any of them might have doctored the tea before the waltz. Slack was already asleep when Pavel arrived."

"Pavel's arrival might very well have saved the B—black trunk," he said, pulling himself short on the last words. "If whoever was in here heard his approach, he might have nipped across the hallway and hidden in a spare room until Pavel went inside."

Miranda did not notice the near slip. "I did not see Laurent," she said. "He might have been in the library. He is always reading the journals to keep abreast of developments at the Congress. You do not suspect Laurent? He is dead set against Bonaparte. His hope is to see Louis back on the throne, so that he can recover his papa's estate."

"But if Bonaparte should win . . ."

"Do not say such things," she said angrily.

"One always has to consider the worst case. If Boney should win, then . . ." He could not say more without telling her what was in the trunk, but the

contents of that trunk might very well be repaid by
the return of the Valdor estate to its rightful owner.
In fact, what he had stolen was much more valuable if Bonaparte won. God, what sort of idiot was
he to have taken it? He had to get it returned, at
once.

It was odd he had not heard from Castlereagh.
Even the redoubtable Castlereagh was uncertain
what to do about this situation. Rotham hoped it
had not become a matter for Cabinet discussion at
Whitehall, or the whole of London would know of
his folly. No, Castlereagh was the very soul of discretion. He would tell no one, and if the truth
leaked out, he would deny it categorically as an underhanded Whig rumor.

Rotham's gaze turned to Miranda, where he saw
another victim of what Society called his high spirits. When had he become such a fool? Not content
with creating a potential international incident, he
had offended a guest in his house, a neighbor, and
a family who had been friends of his family forever.
Done it as petty revenge for her innocent prank.

"I am sorry about—what happened in Papa's
study," he said, suddenly grave. "That was unfor-
givable."

"Indeed it was," she agreed at once, "but at least
it was not serious." Rotham breathed a small sigh
of relief. Good, she was not a Bath Miss, to make a
mountain of one stolen kiss. "Why do you not get
the black trunk off to London, Rotham? It is obvious that someone knows it is here and is after it."

He thought a moment before replying. "I felt it
was more vulnerable on the road than locked up in
my room. Besides, it would only have to be re-

turned eventually. I am waiting to hear from Castlereagh."

"What is the secret about it? The old linen itself cannot be of much value," she said. "I could do better stitchery myself. Is there a message embroidered on it?"

"Something like that. I believe I shall ask Cook to come up," he added, to forestall further questions.

He pulled the cord, which brought a kitchen servant, who goggled to see Miss Vale sitting as calm as a kitten in his lordship's sitting room. She got only a glimpse of her over Rotham's shoulder, for he met her at the door. He did not want to frighten her with a view of Slack's comatose body. She agreed to send Cook up.

Cook was a heavyset woman who did not take kindly to being asked to leave her kitchen in the middle of a party, to say nothing of that flight of stairs. Having known Rotham from the egg, she had no fear of him. He met her in his own room, with the sitting room door closed.

"You wanted to see me, your lordship?" she demanded, with a glare that said, "This better be important."

"I am curious to know who asked you to send that supper up to Slack."

"He asked me hisself," she replied, with a belligerent note in her voice.

"He did not go down to the kitchen, I think?"

"Nossir, he did not. He rang the bell. Mary answered and he said he wanted a bite. Well he might, poor soul, locked up in that room night and day like a mad dog. I sliced him up some cold mutton and cheese and a half loaf."

89

"And a pot of tea. Who prepared it?"

"I did myself. Mary brought it up. He had asked her to just knock five times when she came and leave it outside the door, which she did."

"Thank you, Cook. That will be all. Send Mary up, if you please."

Cook waddled off, grumbling into her collar. Mary went hopping upstairs again, feeling extremely guilty. She would not tell his lordship about the little flirtation with the gentleman. No harm in it—he had only stolen a kiss.

"Did you see anyone in the corridor when you left the tray outside the door?" Rotham asked.

"Nossir." She knew something untoward was going on and feared the whole would end up in her dish. Best to lay a trail pointing away from her. "That is—I heard a door open and close, but I did not see anyone."

"Which door?" he asked, his heart pumping.

"That one," she said, pointing behind her, to the door across the hall from Rotham's. "I thought it funny, like, for it's a spare room. There's no one in it, unless you have Mr. Berthier put up there."

"No, Mr. Berthier is around the corner."

"Then it was her," Mary said, her eyes open as wide as barn doors.

The question came out in a bark. "Who?"

"The Blue Lady," Mary said. His hopes went crashing to the ground. "She's walking tonight. Didn't Lord Pavel say something about Miss Vale being frightened by her earlier on? I'm sure he did, when he came running into the kitchen, after we heard her holler—Miss Vale, I mean, for the Blue Lady is silent as the tomb. 'I will see to Miss Vale,' he said. 'It is only the Blue Lady.' And he told us to carry on. It gave me quite a turn, having to bring Slack's tray up, with her on the loose."

Rotham asked a few more questions, but was soon satisfied that Mary had no more to tell. He dismissed her, then went to the door and told Miranda he was leaving for a moment. He would be right across the hall, but he locked the door behind him, just to be safe.

He went to the Green Room across the hall. He should have made sure it was locked earlier. The door was closed. When he opened it, a long triangle of light from the hallway showed him the flower pattern of the pale green carpet. "Is there anyone there?" he called, and waited. No answer came from the darkness beyond. Some sixth sense caused a tingle along his scalp. It was the foolish talk of the Blue Lady. He could go back for a lamp, but he knew there were a lamp and tinderbox by the bedside table not three steps in front of him. He stepped into the darkness, and the room suddenly exploded into a myriad of shooting sparks. As he fell he reached out his hand and felt the smooth, cold softness of a silk skirt. The susurration of silk moving was the last thing he heard until he opened his eyes two minutes later.

Pavel was standing over him with a lighted lamp in his hand. "Rotham! Good God, don't tell me they have poisoned you as well!"

Rotham sat up, rubbing his bruised forehead. He had been hit from in front, the blow catching him between the eyes. He looked around wildly. "Did you see her?" he asked.

"Who?"

"The lady—"

"The Blue Lady? Dash it, Rotham, you know that is a bag of moonshine."

Rotham sat with his hands holding his aching head. "There was a lady waiting in the darkness. She hit me with something." He looked around.

"This would be the weapon, I fancy," Pavel said, lifting something from the floor. He held up a malacca cane, dark brown, mottled with a lighter brown. Its gold cap was embossed around the edge with a gadroon.

Rotham had seen it before. It was Berthier's cane. But it was not Berthier who had struck him, unless he was wearing a lady's skirt. He struggled to his feet, shaking away the residual stars that still danced before him.

"Let us have a look around to see if anything else was left behind," he said.

He and Pavel toured the room, but the intruder had left no more clues.

"I say, Rotham, where is Miranda?"

"She is with Slack."

"Then we had best join her. It is not pleasant work for a lady, guarding him. It made my flesh crawl, I can tell you. He looked like a corpse."

Miranda had not been disturbed during their absence. She noticed at once that Rotham was pale and demanded to be told what had happened.

"Someone coshed him on the head," Pavel announced, pleased to have such important news to impart.

Miranda was equally excited to hear it. "Really!" When she saw Rotham's dark look, she added, "I hope it did not hurt much. You can have Dr. Makepiece look at it when he comes. Did you see who struck you?"

"No, but it was a lady."

Pavel held out the cane. "We fancy this was the weapon."

"That suggests a gentleman, yet a gentleman does not use a cane inside the house," she said. "There would be plenty of weapons as good in the Green Room—the poker, for instance. Odd that the cane was used. Do you recognize it, Rotham?"

"It is Berthier's cane," he said, "but as you pointed out, it is odd it was brought up to that room, unless the intention was to leave it behind as a clue."

"That don't make sense," Pavel frowned. "Why would Berthier want you to suspect him?" Then he gave a sheepish grin. "Heh, heh—what they call a red herring, you mean. Someone else left it behind to incriminate Berthier. Dashed scoundrel."

"Was anyone missing from downstairs?" Rotham asked him.

"The deuce of it is, the dancing had just finished, and everyone was milling about, some to the refreshment parlor, some of the ladies was coming upstairs to tend to their toilettes, and some of them was coming down."

"Which ladies were coming down?" Rotham asked.

"That is hard to say. Of the ones you asked about in particular, Louise was stopped on the stairs chatting to Mrs. Dumont. I could not very well ask her whether she was going up or down, and I did not like to wait to see, for I knew you was anxious about Madame Lafleur and the others."

"Was Madame Lafleur at the card table? I thought she was headed that way."

"No, but neither was anyone else, except Papa

and Sir Alfred Sykes, and they was only discussing the Corn Laws. Mama had taken a group of the ladies to the Tapestry Room to show them *Ashmead*, the piece she is working on, you know. By the time I ran them to ground, Madame Lafleur was just going into the room, a little behind the others."

"All of this is not much use," Miranda said, looking to Rotham to see if he could make sense of it. She noticed a bump was forming in the middle of his forehead, just between his eyes. It looked so very odd, as if he were growing a horn. A smile tugged at her lips.

Pavel noticed what she was looking at and laughed. "Dash it, Rotham, you have a bump the size of an onion blossoming from that hit. You look like a unicorn. Take care or some virgin will get her clutches on you."

Rotham touched the bump and winced. "What the devil are you talking about?"

"The old myth about the virgin and the unicorn. You know, the one on the tapestry. Oh, never mind. Where were we? We have not eliminated any of our suspects, including Berthier and Laurent," Pavel said. "If it was Laurent, and he took Berthier's cane to direct suspicion on him, then it is four pence to a grout he was sly enough to bring along a shawl as well, to let on it was a skirt. The only one it eliminates is Berthier. He would not be fool enough to bring his own cane."

"I disagree," Miranda said at once. "He would not plan to leave it behind. He probably dropped it in the excitement. I do not exclude Berthier by any means, although the silken skirt certainly suggests a lady. Did it feel like a skirt, Rotham, or might it have been a shawl?"

"It felt like a skirt. It was a lady. The flesh beneath the silk was softer than a man's body. Of course, there might have been a lady and a man together."

"So, what is to do?" Pavel asked.

"I shall stay with Slack until the doctor comes," Rotham said. "You two go belowstairs and see if you can learn anything. You might ask Boxer if he saw anyone take the malacca cane from the Chinese jar in the front hall where they are left, Pavel."

"And I shall hint around to Louise and Madame Lafleur to see if I can learn anything," Miranda added.

"No, we do not want them to know they are suspected," Rotham said. "If they are guilty, they will lie regarding their whereabouts. Act as if nothing had happened, but keep your ears and eyes open. You might overhear something."

This job was better than nothing, and it had the added advantage of allowing them to enjoy a late-night supper. They left Rotham to await the doctor's arrival and went belowstairs. Boxer had not seen anyone remove a cane from the Chinese jar. It seemed highly suspicious that the four suspects sat at the same table. As all the seats at that table were filled, Miranda and Pavel were forced to sit at the other side of the room, consoling themselves that the guilty parties were not likely to discuss their plans in such a public venue.

It was not until the supper was over that anything out of the ordinary happened. Berthier walked up to them and said, "I did not see Rotham at supper. I hope he is not ill?"

Miranda studied him for signs of guilt. Neither his silver temples nor his brown eyes gave a thing away. He looked disgustingly innocent, even concerned.

"He has a touch of headache," Pavel said. "Walked into a door, actually," he added, to account for the lump on his forehead.

Berthier gave a sharp look. "Has he retired? I wanted a word with him."

"I believe he has, yes," Pavel replied.

"I daresay it can wait until morning. It was a nice party. We did not manage a dance, Miss Miranda."

"No."

"Another time. How are your mama and papa?"

"Fine, thank you."

"And the baroness?"

"Trudie is fine, too."

"Good. Well, I shall say good night to Lady Hersham. I am ready for the feather tick."

As soon as he left, Miranda said, "What does he want with Rotham? Did you notice the sneaky look he gave when you mentioned your brother had walked into a door?"

"Had to say something to account for that lump. I shall nip up and warn him what I told Berthier."

Miranda loitered about the saloon as the guests took their leave. Louise and Laurent were saying their farewells to Madame Lafleur. Miranda wandered close to them to listen.

"We shall call tomorrow to discuss plans for Brighton," Louise was saying to madame. "Or if I cannot go, I shall send a note with Laurent."

"He will not want to come without you," madame said, smiling at Laurent in a very knowing, French way.

Louise was always pleased to have her desirability flaunted. She was so sure of her attractions that she could even deny them. "It is all a hum, Laurent's devotion to me," she said. "When we are alone he speaks nothing but politics."

"You don't fool me," madame said dutifully. "I smell the April and May."

Louise mentally added this bit of broken English to her repertoire. Madame was an excellent source of such gems.

Miranda lingered until madame was seen off, but learned nothing of the least interest. As it was late, she said good night to her hostess and went upstairs. At the top of the steps, Pavel was waiting for her.

"He went to Rotham's room—Berthier I mean—after I told him Rotham had gone to bed."

"Did Rotham let him in?"

"He welcomed him with open arms. I dropped by a moment later and tapped five times on the door, gave the password, just to make sure Berthier was not murdering my brother. Rotham told me everything was fine, and I should go to bed. It seems he trusts Berthier."

"Or is pumping him for information," Miranda added.

"I believe I shall just wait a bit in the Green Room across the hall. Better safe than sorry, eh?"

"A good idea."

Miranda wanted to stay in the Green Room, too, for she disliked to miss a moment of the excitement, but fatigue overcame her, and she went to her bedroom. She smiled at the unicorn, thinking of Rotham and the lump on his forehead. He did not even know the myth about the unicorn and the virgin.

Chapter Nine

A late night did not keep Miranda from being at the table bright and early the next morning. To her dismay, Pavel was not there to tell her what had come of Berthier's visit to Rotham's chamber the night before. Only Laurent was there. After filling her plate, she gamely set about quizzing him to see what she could learn. She still found him dangerously attractive. There was something about his French accent and dark, brooding eyes that reminded her of the heroes of gothic novels—a sense of passion lurking beneath the civil veneer.

"Did you enjoy the rout last night, Laurent?" she asked.

"Un peu," he said. He occasionally slipped into French when he was distracted, as he appeared to be on this occasion. "Though one feels guilty dancing while all of Europe is on the edge of chaos."

Oh, dear, he was going to preach politics to her. "I expect we shall hear of Wellington's victory any day now," she said, hoping to derail him.

"I trust it may be so. There are some, even among us, who will not be happy if it happens," he added gloomily.

"Surely you are mistaken," she replied.

"I was surprised to see Monsieur Berthier had

been invited to visit at Ashmead. He is not a close friend of the family. I hear from friends in Rye that Berthier takes frequent trips. He does not say where, but perhaps it is back to his home in France, *non*? I fear this new closeness between him and Rotham. Rotham, alas, has never been known for his judgment."

Miranda felt a sting of annoyance at the charge, although she knew it to be well earned. "As Lord Castlereagh and the Duke of Wellington trust Rotham, I think we may rest easy on that score," she replied coolly.

"I trust we may, yet if he should—waver in his allegiance to England, he is in a position to do irreparable harm. He speaks highly of Bonaparte."

"The most loyal of Englishmen acknowledge Bonaparte's skill, I believe."

"That is so, yet you recall that Rotham visited Bonaparte at Elba and was inordinately impressed with him."

"Rotham was sent to Elba by the government!"

"True, yet it is possible that great harm was done by the visit. Rotham would not be the first young gentleman to be seduced by a heroic warrior. The pages of history are littered with such accounts. I am happy that Rotham was sent home from Vienna. He can do little harm here."

The words "sent home" implied misconduct on Rotham's part. It was indeed odd, and as she considered it, she was not happy that he had brought Berthier to Ashmead at this time.

"He was sent to England to consult with Castlereagh," she said.

"Yet he does not consult. He does not go to London, nor do many dispatches from Whitehall arrive for him. He has instead a rout party. It is very strange. Do not take my little warning amiss, Miss Vale. I think only of your happiness." He looked at her with his sad, sultry eyes and said, "I would not like to see you hurt, *ma petite*."

"I do not see how his behavior can hurt me," she said. His sultry eyes began to work some magic on her. She saw that Rotham's behavior in purely social circumstances had been of the sort that could hurt her, if she were so foolish as to go falling in love with him.

"A word to the wise—that is what you *anglais* say, *non?*"

She acknowledged it with a tacit nod. Laurent sipped his coffee, then continued in a gentle, apologetic way.

"I have offended you by my interference. I am extremely sorry. It is concern that forces me to speak. I see a growing friendship between you and Rotham. No doubt he has told you some story to account for Berthier's presence at this time?"

Miranda realized she was being quizzed, but as she had no idea why Berthier was here, she could not have told him even if she had wanted to, and she did not want to. "You overestimate my closeness to Rotham. He has said nothing to me."

"*Eh bien*, it stands to reason he would not reveal any unwise doings to a young lady he hopes to impress." Then he set aside his napkin and rose. A dazzling smile had suddenly appeared, adding the final touch of beauty to his countenance. "Comtesse," he said, with a graceful bow. "Allow me to get your breakfast."

"I had breakfast in bed," Louise replied. She said, "*Bonjour*, Miss Miranda," then turned at once to continue speaking to Laurent. "You have not forgotten we must go to Rye this morning? I have dozens of things to pick up before we go to Brighton. I have an appointment with Mademoiselle Chêne. She was to begin work on my new gown yesterday. If we get an invitation to the prince's pavilion, I shall wear it. Lady Hersham agrees it would be convenient if Mademoiselle Chêne came to stay at Ashmead while my gown is being made up."

"We can bring her from Rye with us," Laurent said, always eager to please the comtesse.

"I shall call on Madame Lafleur as well." She turned to Miranda. "Will you tell Lady Hersham not to hold luncheon for me? We may take lunch with Madame Lafleur. She mentioned something about it last night."

"I shall tell her," Miranda agreed.

"You will excuse us now, ma'm'selle," Laurent said to Miranda.

As they left the room, she heard him telling Lousie she must take along a parasol. He spoke French in a soft, loving tone, most of which she could understand. "A delicate complexion such as yours—like a newly opened rose—cannot take the blast of the sun, *ma chere*."

The comtesse answered in unaccented English that he was too droll. England had no real sunshine. "You must not pretend you care for me, sly dog. It is no such a thing." Louise did not bother with her linguistic tricks when she was alone with Laurent. Perhaps she assumed English was the proper aphrodisiac for a Frenchman, but her nonchalant manner did not suggest she considered him a potential husband.

Miranda sighed. If Laurent had told her her

cheeks were like rose petals, she felt she could fall in love with him. But he only spoke to her of politics.

It was not until they were gone that Miranda realized she had not managed to ask either of them a single question. She felt uneasy after the meeting with Laurent. The seeds of mistrust he had planted began to sprout. It was true Rotham was an admirer of Bonaparte. She had found it odd, too, that he did not rush off to London. Why was Berthier suddenly visiting at Ashmead? And what was the importance of the mysterious black trunk? It surely had nothing to do with that faded old embroidery. That was only a sham. She was on nettles by the time Pavel joined her, his chest swelling with importance.

"What happened last night?" she demanded as soon as he arrived.

He made her wait until he had helped himself to a piece of roast beef and eggs before obliging her.

"Berthier never left Rotham's room last night. Or at least, he was still there when I began to fall asleep at three o'clock. I went along to my own bed then, for I had a wicked crick in my neck. I crept to the door and tried to peek in the keyhole. I could neither see them nor hear a thing, but I heard the black trunk being dragged along the floor at one point."

"He stayed all night!"

"Until three at least. I plan to run up as soon as I have had a bite. Anything going forth down here? Berthier or Rotham did not come in for breakfast?"

"Not yet. Laurent and Louise were here. They are off to Rye. He said some nasty things before

Louise arrived," she said, and was, of course, asked to repeat them.

Pavel screwed up his face and shook his head. "Dashed Frenchie. That is no way to repay the family's hospitality, telling tales behind our backs. I wish Papa would send him packing. He has been sponging on us forever, letting on he is trying to find a position."

"You do not think it could be true, what he said?"

"Of course not. Dash it, Rotham is an Englishman and proud of it. No denying he has that wild streak. Runs in the family. Uncle Horatio was a thorn in the family's side. Rotham used to wear a white hat when he was a youngster."

"I remember hearing about that white hat. The neighbors were upset about it. What did it mean?"

"The sign of a Republican," Pavel explained. "Supporter of Napoleon. Mind you, that was at the time when the revolution was falling apart, and Boney came dashing home from Egypt to get a grip on things. Plenty of Englishmen was for him at the time. They did not know he would take over entirely and become a tyrant. He was supposed to be setting up a consulate or some such thing. Rotham's Republican phase only lasted one summer, then Papa had him on the carpet. Tossed the white hat in the grate, threatened to cut off his allowance, and we heard no more of Republicanism."

"I remember Rotham was very excited when he was chosen to be part of the delegation sent to Elba."

"Who would not be? It was a great honor. He was the youngest delegate."

"You don't think— No, of course not."

"I don't think he is a traitor, if that is your meaning," Pavel shot back angrily. "Though I wish I knew why he has taken Berthier into his confidence when he won't tell us anything."

"Laurent was quizzing me about Berthier."

They were interrupted by a loud knocking at the front door. It was an emissary from Whitehall with a red dispatch box for Lord Rotham. The box was of sufficient importance that the man would hand it over to no one but Rotham.

Rotham was called down and went into the study with the box, closing the door behind him. He came out twenty minutes later, handed his reply to the emissary, and returned to the study. Pavel and Miranda went at once to ask him what was going forth. Miranda noticed his bump had begun to shrink. It was still visible, but hardly large enough to turn him into a unicorn.

"I have to leave for London this morning," he announced.

"What about—you know, the black trunk?" Pavel asked. "We shall guard it for you. Or will you be taking it with you?"

"My orders are not to remove it from Ashmead, nor to draw attention to it by arming the place like a fortress. I think—yes, I think Slack and Berthier between them can handle it."

"What about us!" Pavel demanded.

Rotham saw that he must appease these unwanted helpers and quickly invented a job for them. "You know who the suspects are. I count on you to watch them and report to me on their activities."

"But Berthier is one of the prime suspects!" Miranda objected. "You cannot leave the trunk with him."

"You are mistaken. Berthier is helping me."

"I see," Miranda said, narrowing her eyes in Pavel's direction.

"Righto. We shall toddle along and keep an eye on the suspects for you," Pavel said, then he and Miranda left.

When they were beyond the door, he fell into a scowl. "I fear you are right, Sissie. He has turned coat on us."

"We cannot let him do anything foolish. We must stop him."

"Thing to do, have a word with Papa. No point thinking Rotham will listen to me. I had best go alone. Papa will not appreciate my bruiting the story about the countryside."

"I am not the countryside," she objected.

"Still, he will be more forthcoming if we are alone. I shall tell you what he says. I saw him in the rose garden earlier. He rises with the birds."

Pavel went along to the garden, while Miranda went outdoors to stroll through the park. Ignoring the tiered gardens and poplar-lined allée with a Roman statue at its focal point, she chose her direction to coincide with a view of the rose garden. She observed from the shelter of a spreading elm while Pavel and his papa talked for five minutes. Lord Hersham seemed very upset. She caught up with Pavel as soon as he left.

"What did he say?"

"He gave me a regular tongue thrashing. Told me to mind my own dashed business, and if I suggested to a soul that Rotham was a traitor, I would not sit down for a week. He has gone to have a word with Rotham now, before he leaves. I expect we will see the back of Monsieur Berthier before long. Papa would not be so upset if he were not worried to death."

They watched from a distance as Lord Hersham hurried toward the house. "That is that, then," Pavel said. "Shall we get on with watching the suspects?"

"Let us wait and see what Rotham does after your papa has a word with him. I expect we will see Berthier turned off."

They darted back into the house and took up a position outside the study door. They could hear voices speaking in low, confidential tones, but it was clear that Hersham was not ringing a peel over his elder son. When they heard footsteps approach the door, they hastened into the library and waited until Lord Hersham's footsteps receded into the distance.

"As Laurent and Louise are going into Rye, I shall call for the gig," Pavel said, and went to arrange it. "You can keep an eye on things here."

Miranda remained in the library alone, thinking. She did not believe Rotham would go against his papa's wishes in the matter at hand. And if he would not disoblige his papa, how could he betray his country? Lord Hersham's loyalty was not in question. Yet Laurent's words kept replaying inside her head. What had begun as an exciting spy game had become painfully serious. She felt a heavy ache in her heart to think of dashing, handsome Rotham being a traitor, ending his days at the end of a silk rope. Peers, she had heard, were hung with a silk rope—aristocrats still, even on the gallows.

"Why so sad, Miranda?" a voice said from the doorway.

She turned at the sound of Rotham's voice and

studied him with a disillusioned eye. He looked as he had always looked. His life of crime had not yet carved its inevitable ravages on his handsome face.

"What are you going to do, Rotham?" she asked.

"I am leaving for London. I was just looking for you to say good-bye."

"I do not know what rig you are running, but whatever it is, I wish you would reconsider. You are only storing up future misery by the way you are behaving. Think of your family, if you have no concern for your own reputation."

A frown darkened his brow, and when he spoke, his accent was rough. "I have every concern for my reputation, and my family's. Why can you not trust me?"

"How could anyone possibly trust you?"

He felt a wince at her charge, but whether it was anger or shame, he could not decide. "I have been foolish in the past," he admitted, "but I am becoming wiser with age. It will be all right, Miranda. You'll see. Now show me a smile before I leave."

Her sulky pout only increased. She turned her back on him to show her displeasure, waiting for him to come to her. Perhaps he would kiss her good-bye. For a moment she gazed out the window at four Italian statues of cherubs marking the corners of a paved court outside the window. When Rotham said nothing, she turned back to him. He was gone.

The fun had gone out of the game. She would go to Rye with Pavel after all. Hersham could watch Berthier, since he had not turned the man off. She did not expect to learn anything of interest at Rye. The traitor was right here, at Ashmead, and there was not a thing she could do about it.

Chapter Ten

The trip to Rye proved uneventful, and to make the day even worse, a gray sky and strong wind from the sea threatened a storm. Laurent dropped the comtesse off at the modiste's and continued on to visit Madame Lafleur for half an hour. At the end of that time, he had the carriage return to Mademoiselle Chêne's to pick up Louise and the modiste. The latter brought with her a bandbox, holding a nightgown and a change of linen, and a wicker basket, well known to the local ladies to hold the accoutrements of her profession—pattern books, ribbons, laces, buttons, and such things. The conversation between Pavel and Miranda all had to do with Rotham and the black trunk.

Pavel had rethought his position. "If Papa supports Rotham, then Rotham ain't doing anything wrong," he announced. "We have got hold of the wrong end of the stick somehow."

She was happy to hear his opinion, but was not convinced. "If he is not doing anything wrong, why will he not tell us what he is doing?" she countered.

"Because it is a secret, ninnyhammer."

"He has done something horrid, or your papa would not have given him that scolding the day he arrived."

"It was more shock than anything else. The two of them were laughing before the meeting was over, and they have been meeting regularly in Papa's office without arguing as well. When Papa disapproves, he gives one gigantic rant, treats you as if you did not exist for three days, and then it is over. He don't behave the way he is behaving with Rotham now."

They followed Louise's carriage back to Ashmead at a discreet distance. The remainder of the day was a dead bore. Louise spent the better part of the afternoon in her room with the modiste, while Laurent scowled over the journals in the Blue Saloon. Of Berthier they saw nothing except at dinner, which he took with the family while Slack guarded the room. The evening consisted of a quiet game of cards, without Berthier. He had returned abovestairs after taking port with the other men. Miranda began thinking it was time to return home. Rotham had not said when he would be back. He might stay in London for weeks or slip off to Brighton to visit Louise.

The next morning Miranda offered to continue repairs to the old tapestry in the Tapestry Room, while Lady Hersham worked at her high-warp loom. The warp threads were drawn tightly around rollers at the top and bottom of the loom to form a background on which threads of the woof would create the pattern. Lady Hersham checked the cartoon taken from the wedding portrait as she worked at the back of the loom, with a mirror before the tapestry to show her how it looked in front. They were interrupted only once. Louise came to announce she would be leaving for Brighton the next day if that suited Lady Hersham.

"Ma'm'selle is making good time with your gown, eh? That is excellent, Louise. Is it all arranged that Madame Lafleur will accompany you?"

"Laurent settled the details this morning. She is *aux anges*. She does not get many *vacances*. I hope you and Lord Hersham will visit us as well. It is not far—an easy day's travel. I shall notify you if the Prince Regent is there."

"Yes, you do that, dear." Lady Hersham smiled. Under her breath she added, "And we will be certain to stay away!" She knew Louise only wanted her there to attract those callers who would not come to pay their respects to the Comtesse Pierre de Valdor. Poor relatives were such an affliction, especially when they were socially ambitious.

Louise examined the tapestry and uttered exaggerated praise. "Of the most realistic! The horses so—horselike, as if they would gallop out of the loom. Such exquisite stitchery, madam. You are the genius."

"The artist was the genius. I only do the common labor."

"You are too modest. You are creating the masterpiece for posterity. And now I must go. Boxer is having my trunks descended from the attics. Ma'm'selle will do my packings for me, so as not to bother your servants."

Lady Hersham just shook her head when the comtesse left. "The woman is a fool. If she did not make such a cake of herself, she would nab a husband easily enough, for she is really very pretty."

"I think Laurent would like to marry her," Miranda said.

"In a minute, if he could afford her. But then I would not wish him on my worst enemy. A dead bore. He speaks of nothing but politics. That is fit conversation for gentlemen; I should think a Frenchman would have a better notion how to entertain a lady. I duck when I see him coming toward me with that inevitable frown on his face. But I should not complain. Perhaps my sons would be the same if they had had Ashmead pulled out from under them. Life is very hard for Laurent."

They gossiped as they worked. It was the custom for Boxer to bring Lady Hersham tea in mid-morning, as he did on that occasion. It was while she was pouring the tea that Miranda saw Louise in the park. Before the comtesse had walked ten yards, Laurent was rushing out after her. They strolled toward the pavilion, situated on the top of a rolling hill to give a view of the sea beyond. Miranda glanced out again a moment later and saw Laurent struggling to pull Louise into his arms. A little tussle ensued, before Louise allowed him to embrace her in what Miranda considered a shocking manner. Miranda looked away hastily, embarrassed.

That kiss brought back vivid memories of Rotham's attack in the study. She was trying very hard to forget it, but it came to her at odd moments, always causing a heat to invade her. She was happy that Lady Hersham had not seen Louise and Laurent. It was indiscreet of them to choose such a prominent spot for their tryst. The pavilion was visible from a dozen windows. Anyone might see them.

After a morning spent sitting down, Miranda agreed to go for a ride with Pavel in the afternoon. They rode through the park and spinney, down to the seashore. Andy Macpherson's ship was just setting out for France. She wondered if Rotham had taken Castlereagh's brandy to him, or if he had ever been asked to take it. They dismounted to walk along the shingle beach, with the cold wind blowing in off the sea. It snatched at her skirt and blew little balls of foam up onto the shingle, disturbing the horses.

"What have you been doing all day?" Miranda asked, in a desultory manner.

"I have been keeping an eye on the comings and goings in Rotham's room. I am a bit worried, after that drugged tea Slack was served. I notice Ma'm'selle Chêne takes her meals in the kitchen. It would be easy enough for her to slip a bit of powder into the teapot. I had a word with Cook. Rotham had already warned her to be on the qui vive."

"Louise and Laurent are leaving tomorrow for Brighton."

"That would explain why Laurent was in the attic."

"Yes, Boxer was to bring Louise's trunks down. Very likely she sent her slave up to tell Boxer which trunks are hers. They were kissing in the park."

"She is not quite the thing, when you come down to it. Pretty as can stare, but too fast by half. I say, you ain't going to spend the evening in the Tapestry Room, I hope? I have got a dandy new word game for us to play. You make up little cardboard squares of all the letters, and each gets seven cards."

Miranda let him rattle on. The visit had become very flat since Rotham's departure. When they returned to the house, Berthier was belowstairs in the Blue Saloon, talking to Lord Hersham. This was not a major excitement. Berthier and Slack took turns guarding the trunk. In fact, Berthier usually took his meals with the family. He and Lord Hersham had struck up an unlikely friendship, based on their common interest in sheep.

Miranda assumed the book they were poring over was a farmer's almanac, until Berthier said, "Oh, quite! The stitchery is exactly—"

As she glanced at the book, Hersham snapped it shut and set a newspaper over it. "Ah, back from your ride. Where did you go?" he asked in a strained way.

Pavel told him, which left Miranda's mind free to consider what they had been looking at. It was a picture of men in pointy hats, like those on the embroidered linen in the black trunk.

"Why do you not get Sissie a glass of wine, Pavel?" Lord Hersham said. Then he rose, taking the book with him, and said to Berthier, "If you have a moment free, Berthier, I wish you will come into my study. I would like to ask your opinion about a pair of rambouillets Lord Melcher is trying to sell me. Excellent wool. He brought them from France, but they were bred from Spanish merinos."

Berthier rose and bowed to Miranda before leaving.

As soon as they were gone, she said, "They were looking at a picture of the old linen embroidery."

"Eh? Where did they get it?" he said, handing her a glass of wine.

"It was in that book your papa took away."

"Rubbish. There has not been time to get it painted and into a book. Rotham only brought it home a few days ago."

"But it was the same one. I am sure of it. You re-

114

member all those men in pointy hats. And they had circles on their clothing, too. The thing must be famous if it is in a book."

Pavel took a sip of his wine. "Thing to do—get a peek at the book. I think I have got it figured out now."

"What is it?" she demanded.

"The thing was famous before Rotham stole it."

"Obviously. But how can we see it? Your papa took it to his study."

"Never locks his door. Let us run along and see if he has left it open now. We might hear something."

They went into the hallway, around the corner, and down the corridor to Lord Hersham's study. They could see from the end of the corridor that the door was open. The windows cast a patch of light on the floor by the open door. But when they reached the study, it was empty. They searched the desk for the book; it was not there.

"Now that is deuced odd!" Pavel exclaimed.

"Ask Boxer where they went."

Boxer had no hesitation to inform Lord Pavel that his lordship had gone abovestairs with Mr. Berthier.

"They are checking the book against the embroidery!" Miranda exclaimed. "I was right! That was a picture of the embroidery they were looking at. What can it be?"

"If Papa brings the book down again, I shall keep an eye to see where he hides it. One thing it cannot be is a secret message. I mean to say, if it is old as the hills, it can have nothing to do with Boney."

They gnawed over this new aspect of the puzzle until it was time to change for dinner.

Pavel said out of the side of his mouth as he led

Miranda in to dinner, "Papa brought the book down with him. Locked it in his study. I shall take a nip outside after dinner and see if by any chance he left a window open. Not likely. He hates a draft, and that wind is rising."

Berthier dined with the family again, but of course, no word was mentioned of the book. The ladies went to the Blue Saloon while the gentlemen had their port. Louise soon excused herself to go and speak to Ma'm'selle Chêne. "My new green gown is proving *très difficile*," she explained. "I want the fitting to be just right. You will excuse me, madam?" she said to Lady Hersham.

"Of course, Louise. Miranda can entertain me."

She proceeded to entertain herself by falling into a gentle doze by the cozy grate.

She did not awaken when Pavel darted in to say in a low tone, "Wouldn't you know it, Papa's window is closed tight as a drum. He is in his study now. Laurent claimed to have a megrim and went to his room. I believe I shall go and have a word with Papa. What could I use for an excuse?"

"If he is examining the book, he will only close it. We already know what it contains."

"That is true. I shall get a cardboard to make the letters, then."

That was how they passed their evening. The only small consolation was that Pavel was such a poor speller that Miranda won two shillings. At eleven Lady Hersham awoke and announced that it was time to retire. Miranda accompanied her upstairs.

"Tomorrow we shall have another go at the tapestries," Lady Hersham said.

The morrow promised to be another dull scald.

"That will be nice," Miranda said dutifully. She would go home tomorrow. Sukey's spots must be gone by now. But Wildwood would be dull, too, without Rotham. Perhaps Trudie would invite her to visit. She had spoken of finding a *parti* for Miranda.

Chapter Eleven

Miranda usually slept soundly, but that night she was restless. It was not only the strange bed and the mysterious doings at Ashmead that troubled her rest. She felt some deeper discontent that she did not care to examine, lest she find traces of Trudie's folly harbored in her own heart. When she first heard it, she thought it was only a cat or a mouse. As the scratching persisted, growing louder, she realized it was someone outside her door. Her heart pounded. Was it a spy? Was someone going to kill her? She leapt out of bed and grabbed her dressing gown around her without saying a word.

A whispering hiss sounded at her door. "Sissie, it's me!"

Pavel! Her tense shoulders relaxed. She opened the door, and he slid in. "Light a lamp," he said. "I have got news!"

Her fingers shook as she lit the bedside lamp. "What is it?" she demanded. "You frightened me to death."

"Berthier has been murdered!" Pavel said, in a strange, strangled voice.

"What! Pavel, if this is some joke—"

"No, it is true." She noticed then that he was pale and trembling. "I went to check out the Green

118

Room before retiring. Best to be sure, after what happened last night. All was quiet, but I decided I would stay there to stand guard and keep an eye on Slack and Berthier. Eventually I dozed off. It is nearly morning after all. I am not an owl. When I awoke, I decided to go to my own bed. As soon as I went into the hallway, I saw Rotham's door was ajar. Berthier's body was there on the floor, covered in blood."

"What did you do?"

"I woke Slack, then I came here to tell you," he said, in a dazed voice.

"You must tell Lord Hersham."

"Yes, I must," he agreed. Sharing the horror with someone had helped him to recover. "Papa will wonder how I know. I mean to say—not that there is anything wrong in my standing guard. I was only trying to help."

"Tell him, at once! Are you sure Berthier is dead? Might he be drugged, as Slack was?"

They ran together down the hall to Lord Hersham's bedroom.

"He is covered in blood," Pavel said. "And Slack slept through the whole thing. He felt pretty foolish I can tell you, lying there sawing logs while Berthier was done in. He said he did not hear a sound, not so much as a shout, and he is a light sleeper. Someone convinced Berthier to open that door and ran a knife through his ribs before the poor bleater could utter a word. We know one thing now. Berthier is not the culprit."

Miranda remained outside the chamber while Pavel went in and jiggled his papa awake. Unlike Slack, Hersham was a heavy sleeper. Miranda could hear his stertorous snores through the door.

She heard him exclaim, "Pavel! What the devil! It is still dark out. Is Ashmead burning down?"

"It is Berthier, Papa. Someone has killed him."

"Good God! Did they get the tapestry?"

Tapestry? He obviously meant the linen embroidery. Miranda would not have called it a tapestry.

"I don't know," Pavel said, on a curious note.

Fancy his not thinking to check the black trunk. But then a bleeding body would be a great distraction, she allowed. Within seconds Hersham came pelting out of the bedroom, wearing a pair of blue knitted slippers and pulling a burgundy silk dressing gown around him. He was wearing a makeshift nightcap formed by knotting four corners of a handkerchief. And he still managed to look daunting.

"Sissie?" he said, in a bewildered way when he saw her, but he did not wait to question why she was there.

They all three hastened along to Rotham's chamber. Slack stood at the open doorway, wearing a fearful face.

"I am sorry, your lordship," he said. "It was Berthier's shift. I did not hear a thing."

"Is it gone?" Hersham demanded.

Slack turned and looked at the trunk. Its lid was raised, showing a faded paper lining, and nothing else. "He got away with it," Slack said.

"When did it happen?"

"I was to take over at five. Pavel woke me at four-thirty, and I discovered . . ." He looked at Berthier's body.

Miranda just glanced at the empty trunk, then espied Berthier. Slack had drawn his body a few feet into the room. The stains covering his waistcoat might have been molasses; they looked dark and sticky. The knife was not left behind. She saw a pistol on the floor beside him, but obviously he had not had time to use it.

Hersham rushed forward and began examining Berthier. "He is still breathing," he said. "Pavel, run for the doctor. We might manage to save him. He is our only hope of discovering who did this."

Pavel darted off. Hersham was so upset he still did not question Miranda's presence. He and Slack discussed what could be done for Berthier.

"Best not to move him any more," Slack said. "I had to move him a little to get the door closed."

"Put a blanket over him at least. You don't think we might get a spoon of brandy into him?"

"I tried that. He is too far gone. I am sorry, milord."

"It is not your fault, Slack. You did your best. This is my son's doing," he said grimly. Then he looked and really noticed Miranda for the first time.

While Slack got a blanket and wrapped it tenderly around Berthier, Hersham frowned in confusion at Miranda. Before he could speak, she said apologetically, "Pavel woke me."

"Demmed idiot. What did he want to bring a lady into this gruesome business for? What was he doing up in the middle of the night himself, come to that?"

"He was trying to help. He was watching from the Green Room across the hall."

Hersham's eyes lit up at this. "Did he see—"

"He fell asleep," she said in a small voice.

Hersham turned to Slack. "You must set out for London at once to notify Rotham of this. We have got to get it back." He gave another frown in Miranda's direction. "Run along to bed, missie," he said.

She was extremely loath to leave. "I might be of some help to Dr. Makepiece, if he requires boiling water or something of that sort," she suggested.

"Yes, yes, that is true. Run downstairs and boil us up a kettle. Best not to awaken the servants. What a visit for you, poor girl. You might fetch some bandages and basilicum powder, whatever you think— Never mind. Makepiece will bring that with him. My mind is all at sixes and sevens."

Miranda took a lamp and went downstairs into the dark hallway. A tremble seized her as she took her first pace into the gloom. At the back of her mind there hovered the image of Berthier, lying with the blood oozing from his chest. His attacker might be down here, waiting in the shadows. . . . Hersham would not want anything to happen to her. She was about to run back upstairs when she heard a key turn in the front door. He was back! Whoever had stabbed Berthier was returning to the scene of his crime. And he would surely kill her next. Her mind told her to run, but her body refused to move. She was frozen to the spot. The lamp shook in her hand. It took all her efforts to blow out the flame. Perhaps he would not see her in the darkness. If she stood very still, she might identify the intruder.

But it was too late. He had seen the light from her lamp and was coming rapidly toward her. She could see it was a man, tall, walking quickly, right toward her. The fear of imminent death brought her an instant of sanity. She turned and began running upstairs. In two strides he had caught up to her. She felt his hands clutch at her dressing gown, pulling her back down. Just as she opened her mouth to scream, a hand was clamped over it. With his other arm, he pulled her roughly against him, her back pressing against his chest.

"So it is you, after all," he said in a grim voice. Rotham's voice! The echo of her heartbeat inside her ears was so loud she could hardly hear him, but she recognized the familiar voice, and a wave of relief washed through her. She tried to turn, but he held her too tightly to move.

"I am going to remove my hand from your lips now, Comtesse. I doubt you will want to call attention to yourself by shouting. You have some explaining to do."

He removed his hand, but still held her from behind. She took a deep breath and said faintly, "It is me, Rotham. Miranda."

He turned her around in his arms and peered down into her shadowed face. By the wan ray of moonlight from the window, he discerned that it was indeed Miranda Vale. His mood changed from anger and vigilance to something softer. He thought she looked quite adorable, with her raven curls in disarray and her large, dark eyes gazing at him. He could not imagine what she was doing belowstairs at such an hour, but he was heartily glad to see her. He had been thinking of her during the journey and cursing himself for an idiot. Bad enough he had the Trudie affair to overcome, now this tapestry business.

"Planning to make off with the family silver, were you?" he joked.

"No, I came to boil water."

"As none of the servants is enceinte, it cannot be

123

a birthing that requires boiling water. Excellent. We shall have a tea party, and you shall tell me how much you missed me."

How could he joke at a time like this. She wanted to hurt him and said bluntly, "Berthier has been stabbed. The tapestry is gone."

He just stared at her, unable to speak. His first reaction was that it was a bad joke, to repay him for frightening her. But as she stared at him, he read the seriousness in her eyes.

He uttered a low moan. "Oh, God! This is all my fault."

"Your papa is with him now. Slack was just preparing to go to London to tell you."

Without speaking, he dropped his arms and ran up the stairs two at a time. Miranda followed him. She knew all this was Rotham's fault, yet she could not find it in her heart to abuse him at this time. He looked so very tired and sorry—and he had looked so happy to see her. She left the father and son alone and went to the sitting room to ask Slack to accompany her belowstairs as she was too shaken to go alone.

"Rotham has arrived home, so you will not have to go after him," she explained.

Slack seemed happy to put off the moment of meeting Rotham and went belowstairs with her.

The dark rooms did not seem at all frightening, with Slack to keep her company. They lit a few lamps as they progressed toward the kitchen. Slack was so remorseful and so full of apologies that he continued apologizing, even to Miranda.

"If I had had the least notion— After what happened to me the other night, I should have stayed awake to watch over Berthier. And even if his lordship can recover the tapestry, who can take it back?"

"The tapestry?" she asked, hoping to learn at last what had been stolen.

Her question brought Slack back to attention. "I'll stoke up the fire, if you will fill the kettle. We could all use a cup of tea, eh? In fact, I feel a glass of wine would not go amiss tonight, though I am an abstainer. Let us have a tipple of Cook's sherry. She will not mind."

He went to the cupboard and brought out the bottle. Miranda declined, but Slack felt the need of a medicinal glass of spirits and swallowed the whole glassful in one gulp, before stoking up the fire. Cook had already filled the kettle before retiring, so Miranda made up a tray of teacups, milk, and sugar. The kitchen was as familiar to her as the kitchen at Wildwood. Many the cup of tea and gingerbread she had been served here by Cook when she was young. She attempted a few more questions while waiting for the water to boil, but Slack was on his guard and revealed nothing new.

"You will read about it soon enough in the journals," he said ominously. "Until then, it ain't my place to speak."

They were just taking the tea tray and the basin of hot water upstairs when Pavel and Dr. Makepiece arrived. They went upstairs together in a column, Slack leading the way. Makepiece went immediately to the patient. He cut Berthier's shirt open and examined the wound, muttering about severe loss of blood and a weak pulse. "It is not likely he will pull through," he said dolefully, "but I shall do what I can."

Slack and Rotham gently lifted him onto Rotham's

bed and watched while Makepiece bathed away the blood and administered to the wound. Berthier lay pale and still as death throughout.

Miranda poured tea and passed it around. Lord Hersham reached for Rotham's bottle of brandy and added a tot to each cup. Diluted with the tea, Miranda found the brandy welcome on this occasion. It eased the tension that held her tight.

Rotham and Slack had moved to a corner of the room where they spoke in low tones. Miranda moved a step closer to overhear what was being said.

"Did he speak at all?" Rotham asked.

"Not a word. I don't know how long he had been lying there. Lord Pavel woke me at four-thirty. I went to take a look. There he lay on the floor. I should have kept him company."

"This is not your fault, Slack," Rotham said. "I am to blame for everything. If Berthier dies, it is my damned foolishness that has killed him."

"And we will never know who took—" Slack looked over his shoulder to the empty trunk.

Makepiece announced that he had done all he could do for the present. He would stay with his patient, if the others would be so kind as to leave him in peace and quiet.

It was Hersham who said they would all go belowstairs. No one tried to send Miranda to bed when she tagged along behind with Pavel. She had discovered that if she said nothing, no one paid her any attention, except Rotham. His eyes turned to her from time to time. They wore a sad, questioning look.

In the Blue Saloon the lamps were lit; the gentlemen had a glass of brandy, and Miranda had sherry.

"The important thing now is to try to recover the tapestry," Hersham said to Rotham. "Is it possible it is still in the house? Boxer was given orders to make sure all doors and windows were locked. How could anyone have gotten in?"

Slack was eager to atone for what he considered his lapse. "I'll take a run around and check," he said.

Rotham said, "The front door was locked when I arrived."

Slack took a lamp and left to make the tour. Hersham and Rotham moved to the far side of the room, where they stood in earnest conversation until Slack returned to announce that all doors and windows were secure. Of course, he had not checked the occupied rooms.

"It is possible the thing is still here," Hersham said, brightening. "We shall keep a lookout to see it does not leave and conduct a thorough search tomorrow, beginning with the attics. Anything that leaves this house will be examined."

"He might have lowered it out a window," Rotham suggested. "I shall get a lantern and have a look around outside. It might even be lying on the ground. We don't know how long ago he got away with it."

"It is worth a look. Go ahead," Hersham said.

"Me too," Pavel added.

Miranda did not relish the idea of being left alone with Hersham, so she went abovestairs and got dressed. When she returned below, Rotham was just coming in.

"There was no sign of it," he said wearily. "Slack

and Pavel are taking a look to see if anyone is lurking about."

Hersham gave him a look, half of pity, half of anger. "You had best get a few hours' rest, Rotham, and I shall do the same. We cannot do much more tonight. Tomorrow will be a busy day."

"I rested in the carriage en route from London, but I shall have a wash and some breakfast," Rotham said. Then he added, "I am sorry for all the trouble I have caused, Papa."

"Let it be a lesson to you," Hersham said, and left.

Chapter Twelve

When he came in, Slack was given two more jobs: first, to rouse Boxer and ask him to awaken the servants, and second, to dart to Hythe with a message for Macpherson, the smuggler. Slack was to inquire whether anyone had been in touch with him regarding taking a large parcel to France. If so, Mac was to hold the consignment and notify Rotham at once. If he had not been asked, he was to make discreet inquiries among his men on the same matter. Rotham offered a reward of one hundred guineas for the return of the parcel.

It was earlier than the servants usually arose, but they were generally well treated at Ashmead and never objected to making an extra effort in times of crisis. Rotham, Pavel, and Miranda remained in the Blue Saloon, each wrapped up in his or her own thoughts. Rotham looked distraught, but Pavel, being innocent of wrongdoing, was ripe for more excitement.

"The first order of business—after breakfast I mean—is to make a complete search of the house," he said. "From attics to cellar, not a stone will be left unturned. You can leave that to me and Miranda, Rotham. I wager you have more important things to do."

"What else remains for me to do?" Rotham said, staring into the cold grate. "I have done a pretty good job of destroying myself and Papa—to say nothing of Berthier."

And if Bonaparte succeeded in winning, what hay he would make of this business. It was one thing for England to tweak France's nose by running off with a national symbol, but the palm would go to Boney if he recovered it before any use had been made of it. He would put it on public exhibition in Paris, as he had done to inspire his army and the people in 1803 when he was planning his invasion of England. Now it would have an added luster. William the Conqueror had won England for the French. The parallel to be drawn was that England was not invincible; Bonaparte could do the same.

Rotham had stolen the tapestry to prevent its being used in this way. Castlereagh, although he felt obliged to condemn the action, had been secretly thrilled. "By God, Rotham, you are the limit. Boney will not have it to rouse the fever of patriotism in his men this time around. He will look nohow when he finds we have got it. It is as big a coup as if the Frenchies had stolen the Domesday Book. Mind you, when Louis is back on the throne, we must return it in a private, secret way. Guard it with your life."

Castlereagh had said, "When Louis is back on the throne," but of course, he realized as well as anyone that this was still a moot point. Now to have to face the foreign minister and admit the tapestry had been stolen ... He would look not only a fool, but an incompetent besides. Bonaparte was advancing toward Paris. Any day now he would be sending off to the cathedral for the tapestry. What would he do when he discovered it was missing? No rumors of the theft had begun circulating yet.

"So Miranda and I will conduct the search, then?" Pavel asked.

"Yes, thank you, Pavel." Rousing from his reverie, he turned to Miranda and added with a rueful smile, "And you, Miranda. I take it you know what you are looking for?"

His voice had lost its buzzing arrogance. He looked sad and unutterably weary, with purple smudges beneath his eyes. Miranda felt an urge to comfort him, but with Pavel present, all she could do was smile consolingly.

Pavel replied, "Oh, certainly, the old linen embroidery."

"That's right. I forgot you managed a peek the night Miranda saw the Blue Lady and fainted so convincingly."

Rotham assumed they had not recognized the importance of "the old linen embroidery" and was in no hurry to reveal what it was.

Miranda said, "You recall the comtesse and Laurent are leaving for Brighton today, Rotham. Will you search their trunks?"

"Yes, and their rooms. Do it while they are at breakfast. Best have a look around the modiste's room as well. And for God's sake, be careful. Whoever is responsible for this did not hesitate to stab Berthier. Don't let Miranda enter any of their rooms alone, Pavel. Best arm yourself with a pistol."

"By Jove!" Pavel said weakly. This was something like! He darted off to the Armaments Room at once for a pistol.

"What I cannot understand is why Berthier opened the door," Rotham said to Miranda, for this point kept nagging at him. "He knew the danger. He is experienced in this sort of work. He has done a few jobs for Castlereagh in the past, which is why I asked for his help at this time."

She was disappointed. She had hoped for some more personal sort of talk. "The key to your room is missing from your papa's ring, you recall. Berthier had his pistol out, which suggests he was prepared for trouble. Whoever it was must have forced the door open and stabbed him before he could shoot."

"Yes, that could be it. Berthier would hesitate to shoot a lady, though it was not necessarily a lady. Someone might have listened at the door. Hearing nothing, he would assume Berthier and Slack were sleeping and take his chance. It was risky, but then the reward would have been great. He would be a hero in France."

"You thought it was a lady who hit you in the Green Room the other night. And tonight when you came in, you thought I was Louise, I think? You said, 'So it is you, after all,' in a disillusioned way."

"We cannot overlook the comtesse, certainly. She might hope to smuggle the tapestry out in one of her trunks going to Brighton. Mademoiselle Chêne might be involved as well."

"I shall search Louise's trunks thoroughly."

"And her room, to insure she does not remove her clothing and put the tapestry in after you have searched." He looked at Miranda's eager face and knew he could not put her at risk. "Never mind. I shall risk Louise's—and Laurent's—wrath and have their trunks searched as they leave the house. In that way, you need not worry about them. It is too dangerous. I shall have their carriages searched as well, and set my groom to keep an eye on the stable."

"You do not want me to search their rooms, then?"

"No, but you can check the attics and spare rooms along with Pavel. I feel sure the tapestry has already left the house via a window. I know I would get it safely away as soon as possible, if I were doing it."

"How did you steal it in France? It was taken from a cathedral, I think you mentioned?"

"It was not even guarded. It was just hanging there for anyone to see, or take. I waited until nightfall, broke into the church, and walked off with it. Imagine, an heirloom like that being so poorly watched."

"I was imagining your breaking into a church. You really are the limit, Rotham," she said, shaking her head.

Pavel returned, carrying a charged pistol. "All set. Come along, Miranda. Let us grab a bite before we begin. Are you coming to breakfast, Rotham?"

Rotham wanted to explain, to apologize for having robbed a church, but what excuse had he to offer? That he had been foxed hardly improved the situation.

"I must wash up first and look in on Berthier," he said.

The others went off to the breakfast room. Rotham was reluctant to enter his bedchamber as it held the results of his wretched folly. He would turn the room over to Berthier for the nonce and remove to the Green Room. Makepiece announced no change in Berthier's condition. At least he was not worse.

After washing and putting on a clean shirt, Rotham went outdoors to make a complete circuit of the house in daylight, hoping to see some signs of disturbance beneath one of the windows. There had been no rain recently, however, and thus no moist earth to hold a footprint. He went to the stable and examined Louise's carriage carefully. It held nothing it should not. As an afterthought, he checked out his own family's carriages as well, again without finding the tapestry.

"If anyone brings a large parcel to the stable, notify me at once," he said to his groom. "I particularly want to see the Valdors' trunks before they leave. Notify me if they are sent to the stable."

Laurent did not possess a carriage. Louise owned a carriage and team, but hired a driver. When she was visiting the Hershams, she dispensed with him as an economy measure and used one of Hersham's grooms, so there would be no one to tell the Valdors their trunks had been searched.

Of course, it was entirely possible the Valdors were innocent. Laurent was a nobleman after all, and this scheme did not strike Rotham as a female one. Besides, he did not see how they had discovered he had the tapestry. Was it possible Berthier had unwittingly let something slip and someone from outside had gotten in? Perhaps before the doors were locked for the night. Ashmead was a huge house. It would be possible for someone to hide in a corridor or vacant room for a few hours.

Who was the woman who had been lurking in the Green Room? He did not think it was Louise.

She wore a musky scent. He had not noticed it in the Green Room. It might have been Madame Lafleur—she had attended the rout. And she was friendly with both the Valdors and Berthier.

While he performed his tasks, Miranda and Pavel conducted a thorough search of the attics. The dust had been disturbed in the first room, where the comtesse's and Laurent's trunks had been removed. Three rectangles of dustless wood showed where they had recently rested. The two larger trunks belonged to Louise, the slightly smaller one to Laurent, who, alas, did not possess an abundance of finery.

A fine layer of dust covered the rest of the floor. It was clear at a glance that no one had been moving about the attics unless he had traveled on wings. Miranda pointed this out, but Pavel was not fooled by mere common sense.

"He might have taken a flying leap, landing on that pile of awnings from last year's fête champêtre," he pointed out. A striped awning was indeed within range of, perhaps, a particularly agile gazelle. "From there it is a mere hop to that table with the broken leg. That would take him to the second room. Come along. I wager we will find the embroidery in the next room in one of the trunks."

"He would have broken his neck if he landed on that wobbly table," Miranda said.

"Perhaps he brought a bowl of dust up with him to scatter behind him when he was finished, thinking to fool us. Dashed sneak."

This, while patently absurd, was within the realm of possibility, and Miranda allowed herself to be talked into examining not less than four trunks. The contents provided a walk back through the pages of the eighteenth century. There were ladies' sacques and gowns with hoops and panniers in a variety of rich colors and materials. There were quilted petticoats and stomachers made stiff with pasteboard. There were caps, tuckers, and neckerchiefs. Other trunks held gentlemen's clothing. Moths flew out as Pavel lifted a gaudy red coat with a fitted waist and flared skirt. It had large cuffs, turned back and held with buttons. Another trunk held wigs, some of such an enormous size that Pavel said they would require a neck the size of a stovepipe to hold up the weight. After an hour they still had not found any faded linen embroidery.

The search was not a complete waste, however. Pavel found a dandy set of carved wooden soldiers from the days of Queen Anne and a small diamond cravat pin that had been discarded along with a cravat. Whoever had once owned it had obviously been dead for decades. "Finders, keepers," he said, pocketing the diamond.

When they returned to the bedroom floor, Mademoiselle Chêne was just leaving. She was allowed to go without having her wicker basket and bandbox searched as they were obviously too small to hold an embroidery that had filled a whole trunk. As Miranda had been told not to search the Valdors' rooms, she and Pavel began searching the guest rooms. It was a tedious job. Clothespresses had to be ransacked, mattresses lifted, every tapestry—and there was scarcely a guest room without one—checked to see if another "tapestry" was hanging behind it. Beds had to be peered under, and any chest found had to be opened and searched.

It was while they were in the Primrose Room that Louise came to see what was going forth. She found them emptying a blanket chest.

"What on earth is going on, Pavel?" she demanded. "I have heard you racketing about in the attic above my room loud enough to wake up the corpses. Now you are searching all the bedchambers. Is it that you have lost something?"

"Ah, Louise," he said, smiling guiltily. "Wake up the corpses—you mean wake up the dead. Nothing of the sort, heh, heh. Just looking for treasure. You will never guess what we found in the attic. A diamond cravat pin." He showed her the pin as proof of their innocence.

"How it brings back memories. My Pierre had one like it," she said, and went into one of her remembering trances. "What a charming ring it would make," she said, recovering. "A lady's ring," she added, gazing at her hand to make her meaning clear.

"An excellent notion, but I believe I shall wear it in my cravat instead," Pavel replied.

Miranda thought the comtesse looked more annoyed at losing out on the diamond than concerned at their search. "You give me the migraine," she said, touching her index fingers to her two temples. "Try to be less noisome, *s'il vous plaît*." Then she gave her shoulders a Gallic shrug and left, muttering to herself. *"Mon Dieu, ces enfants!"*

"When are you leaving for Brighton, Comtesse?" Pavel called after her. "I am dashed sorry to see you go."

"Bientôt. Après— After lunch," she said, as if catching herself up on slipping into French, although she did not, in fact, recall the French word

for lunch. "I have asked Boxer to take down the trunks and stow them in my carriage. I cannot imagine what keeps him."

This sent Pavel and Miranda rushing belowstairs to alert Rotham that the trunks were about to descend. They found him in the ballroom, lifting the loose ends of various tapestries to see if anything was concealed behind them.

"We had best get to the stables," Pavel said breathlessly. "I have just spoken to Louise. She has asked Boxer to take the trunks to the carriage. Easier to load 'em onto the rig at the front door. Smells fishy to me. She and Laurent plan to leave right after luncheon."

A flash of hope flared in Rotham's eyes. "Let us go," he said, and they all went out by the front door, hurrying.

The trunks were bound up in leather straps, but they were not locked. Louise's trunks contained her gowns and belongings, along with one small but rather valuable statuette of a shepherdess from her chamber, which she had told Lady Hersham she had accidentally broken. She had made humble apologies and offered to pay for it, knowing no payment would be accepted.

"This proves she is a thief anyhow!" Pavel exclaimed. "By Jove, I shall give this back to Mama."

Rotham frowned. "It proves she has no notion we would search her trunks," he said, "and I rather think she would suspect it if she were guilty. Let it be, Pavel. No point letting her know we searched the trunk."

Pavel was reluctant to let her walk away with a family treasure, but in the end, he decided the statuette was an ugly thing. Laurent's thievery was so small as to be almost pitiful. He had hidden a bottle of Hersham's claret in the bottom of his trunk, wrapped up in a magazine, unaware that Lord Hersham kept a well-stocked cellar at Brighton.

They all felt ashamed for him, but no one called him a thief. "Poor bleater," Pavel said. It expressed the mood of them all.

Rotham told the groom to keep watch on the trunks until the carriage left the stable, then they returned to the house for lunch.

Chapter Thirteen

Laurent and Louise sat by the grate in the Blue Saloon awaiting the call to lunch when Miranda came downstairs. Laurent was brooding over a letter. It was unclear whether Louise was helping him brood or remembering her husband. In any case, she wore her sad face. Rotham and Pavel stood apart from them by the window, talking quietly. It was the latter group Miranda wished to join, but for politeness' sake, she stopped for a word with the Valdors in passing. Laurent immediately rose to his feet and showed her to a chair.

"I see your letter has finally come, Laurent," she said. "I hope the news is good." His sullen expression was not necessarily a harbinger of bad news, nor was the letter he held necessarily from the British Museum, although he did not usually receive any mail.

He folded the letter and put it in his pocket. "I did not get the position at the British Museum," he replied. Either anger or disappointment drew sharp lines from his nose to his mouth. "It seems Sir Peter Nugent, Lord Haley's youngest son, has been chosen. A schoolboy, just down from Oxford. I have more knowledge of French art in my little finger than he has in his empty head. I grew up surrounded by the very best of French art. At the château we had half a dozen Poussins and as many Lorrains. Watteau, Fragonard—we had them all. Has Lord Haley's youngest son ever heard of our great French portraitists, I wonder? Rigaud, Nanteuil, Champaigne—mention Champaigne to Sir Peter and he would think you spoke of wine."

Miranda knew that Laurent had left France when he was five or six years old, so for him to speak of growing up at the château was an exaggeration. He would have to have been an extremely precocious child to even remember the paintings. But when she thought of the bottle of wine hidden in his trunk, she felt a wince of pity. "I am sorry you did not get the position," she said, wondering if she could escape to the window before he got at her with his politics.

Louise gave her head a little shake, as if awakening from a deep sleep. "It is really not fair," she scolded. "It is all nepotism. If only you knew more influential Englishmen." Her green eyes slid in Rotham's direction, just as he and Pavel turned from the window.

"You have heard Laurent's sad newses?" she asked, drawing a long face. The brothers joined the group by the grate. "He was refused the position at the musée. *C'est incroyable.* A curator for the French artworks is required, and they choose an English schoolboy. We have just been explaining to Miss Miranda it is all the nepotism. Can you not put in a speech for Laurent, Rotham?"

"She means a word, I believe," Pavel explained.

Rotham replied, "If the position is already filled, then it is highly unlikely I can change officialdom's mind, but I might find something in another department." Laurent's knowledge of French might be helpful in some nonstrategic position, after the Napoleon business was settled.

"It is very kind of you, milord," Laurent said, with a mixture of gratitude and hauteur that revealed his discomfort in taking favors. "I become restless, battening myself on the charity of others for so long. Perhaps if you would give me a few letters of introduction to your influential friends, I might borrow Louise's carriage and go up to London while we are at Brighton. You permit, Louise?"

"What would I use for a carriage while you are gone?" she asked.

"Mama keeps a whisky in Brighton for short drives along the Marine Parade," Rotham told her. "It would be more convenient than your traveling carriage in the city, especially in good weather."

She did not want to appear selfish and gracefully agreed. It might mean hiring a horse to draw the rig, but on the other hand, Lady Hersham's rig would be recognized and perhaps excite curiosity regarding its occupant. "Between us we shall get you fixed up with something, Laurent." She smiled, very much the grande dame.

"I am most grateful," Laurent replied, gazing soulfully into her eyes. "And to you, Rotham," he added.

"That is why friends are for," Louise said.

Like Miranda, Rotham thought of that bottle of wine sequestered in Laurent's trunk and felt sorry for him. Such petty larceny did not suggest an imagination large enough to be responsible for the missing embroidery.

"My pleasure," Rotham said dismissingly, just as Boxer came to summon them for lunch. It seemed

142

he was forever doing favors for Laurent—the loans (never repaid) of small sums of money, the use of a mount or carriage, writing an introduction—yet he was left with the feeling that he was not doing enough.

Louise was in an effervescent mood with the holiday in Brighton to look forward to. When Lady Hersham joined the group, Louise said, "I have not seen Monsieur Berthier today. Has he left?"

A sudden hush fell over the room. Lady Hersham rose to the occasion. "Yes, he was called home. Hersham was disappointed. They were planning to have a look at some sheep today."

"Ah, the darling sheepses and lambs." Louise smiled. "When may I hope to see you in Brighton, Lady Hersham?"

"Not soon, I fear," the hostess replied, and added untruthfully, "I have had a letter from Selena telling me she would like to bring her family to visit in July. There will be preparations to be made." She did not ask when the comtesse would return to Ashmead.

After lunch Laurent accompanied Rotham to his office, where Rotham scribbled up a few letters of introduction. He would send a note off to Castlereagh explaining how he had been more or less forced into writing them. Castlereagh would see that Laurent did not land in any position where he could be a menace. If, on the other hand, Laurent was innocent, he would be happy to help him.

Louise took a tearful farewell of "all her dear friends and Miss Miranda," declaring she would never forget this visit of the most charming.

"You will be stopping at Rye to pick up Madame Lafleur?" Rotham asked.

"She will be joining us tomorrow," Louise replied. "My fault, I fear. I kept Mademoiselle Chêne so busy with my gown, she had not time to finish madame's. We ladies cannot go to Brighton without a new gown," she added gaily. "We would have waited for her, but Laurent—he was most eager to be off. Madame will come on the first coach tomorrow."

A tinge of pink flushed Laurent's swarthy cheeks. "I had hoped I might get the prince to put in a word for me about the position at the museum," he said. "The Duc de Guichet is in Brighton for a few days only, visiting the prince. He is a friend of my family. After receiving my letter this morning announcing the position is filled, I suggested to Louise we could wait and go tomorrow with Madame Lafleur, but Louise wanted to go today. She has already made an appointment with friends for tomorrow morning, I believe."

Miranda noticed that it was, in fact, Louise who insisted on leaving today and was trying to shift the blame to Laurent. Was she eager to escape because she had stolen the embroidery? It seemed pretty fast for them to be traveling unchaperoned. Her hostess obviously disagreed with her.

"No need to wait," Lady Hersham said at once.

"It is the short drive," Louise pointed out. "Madame will not mind going on the coach. She is used to it. And we have your housekeeper to chaperon us, Lady Hersham," she added, with a shrug that suggested a chaperon was a mere formality.

Immediately after luncheon, the comtesse and Laurent set off for Brighton.

Rotham felt uneasy to see them go. They were his chief suspects, yet they were certainly not

144

carrying the tapestry with them. He remembered that silk gown he had felt in the Green Room the night Slack had been drugged. Who was it? Was it possible Madame Lafleur had the tapestry? If so, she had either broken into the house last night and stolen it, slipped it out the window, thence off to Rye—or someone had passed it out the window to her. He felt a tingle of apprehension. He must get a look at madame's trunk before she left Rye. And how the devil could he ask a perfectly respectable lady to open her trunk to be searched? She might even send the thing on ahead of her, today, but he did not think she would dispatch such a valuable item unguarded on the public coach.

He preferred not to bring the constable into it. The tale would be all over the parish before the sun set. His only other recourse was to get into her house and have a look while she slept that night. Meanwhile, he must have someone in Rye to make sure Louise did not pick up the trunk on her way to Brighton. That was another possibility. Slack was assigned the duty. As there had been no word from Macpherson, Rotham decided to pay him a call in Hythe.

"What are you doing this afternoon?" he asked Miranda.

"We shall keep looking for the embroidery," she said, but with lagging interest, now that the suspects had escaped. "What are you doing, Rotham?"

"I have to go to Hythe. I wondered if you would like to accompany me."

"Has it to do with finding the embroidery?" she asked with sharp interest.

"Yes, I want to call on Macpherson. I really should not invite you on such a shabby errand. . . ."

"I should not accept—but I shall," she added with a pert, laughing look. "Must you tell Lady Hersham where you are going? She might not let me accompany you."

He looked abashed. "What am I thinking of, corrupting the innocent by taking you to call on a smuggler? I have done enough harm. I shall go alone."

"It will be all right when I am with you," she said. Her mind was on what Society would think of the visit to a smuggler, and she knew that when a young lady had Lord Rotham for an escort, she would be forgiven much. Indeed, she was hardly expected to behave with perfect propriety. "Will you take your curricle?" she asked eagerly.

"If you like."

"I should like it of all things. I do not often get a ride in a curricle. Only with Parnham occasionally, and he is a wretched fiddler."

"Now there is a facer for me! It is the company of my grays you are seeking, not me."

"Oh, no! What good are the grays without you, Rotham? I could not handle them."

He lowered a brow at her. "That, of course, is much more flattering."

"I would not insult you by offering flattery."

"And you would not compliment me either, wretch!"

"Pavel says you are a complete hand with the grays, and if I agree after our drive, you may be sure I shall compliment you."

"Get your bonnet," Rotham said brusquely, as it was clear as glass he was not going to receive any compliments.

She ran off for her bonnet and pelisse, for the

wind from the sea was cool, even in mid-June. Pavel was given the assignment of watching the doings at Ashmead during their absence. He had a dozen ideas where the embroidery might be hidden and spent the next few hours scouring the cellars and clambering, with great difficulty, over the slippery slate roofs of Ashmead, where he found a pigeon's nest and decided to take one of the eggs to his room to hatch, under the mistaken impression that it would keep warm if he wrapped it in cotton wool.

Miranda enjoyed the drive along the coast in the curricle, with the wind snatching at her pelisse and tossing the sea into white caps. She felt she was queen of the countryside as she was pelted along at sixteen miles an hour, or at least it seemed like it, with Rotham by her side. Everyone they passed turned to stare at them.

"It is odd that Madame Lafleur is not going to Brighton today," she said. "If the embroidery was lowered out the window, she might have it in her trunk."

"That occurred to me as well. I must get a look in her trunk before she leaves."

"How will you do that?"

"I shall break into her house tonight," he announced blandly.

"Excellent! You are awake on all suits, Rotham. Pavel and I will go with you."

"Pavel may accompany me, if he wishes," he replied dampeningly, but he liked her eagerness for a frolic. He wondered if that eagerness had anything to do with himself.

She gave him a bold look. "Perhaps it would be best if I stayed outside to act as a lookout."

"That was not my meaning, Miranda."

She noticed he had stopped calling her Sissie and wondered at it. Did he finally realize she had grown up? "I know, but I would be safer going with you and Pavel than following alone at midnight."

Rotham lifted a dark eye and examined her impish face. "I hesitate to raise a subject I would prefer to forget, but you are not much like Trudie."

"I believe it is because she was the eldest child and was watched over too closely. It is often the way, although it does not seem to have made you cautious at all."

"I have never been accused of an excess of caution," he agreed. "Quite the contrary."

"Whatever possessed you to do it, Rotham, steal the embroidery?"

"Sheer stupidity."

She did not contradict him. "Why is the old embroidery so important? It did not look like anything special."

"The Bayeux Tapestry not special?" he asked, staring.

"Is that what it is!" she exclaimed. "I have heard of it forever. Why, it is famous. I had no notion it was such a shabby-looking thing. I thought it would be like one of your mama's finer tapestries, with gold threads and things."

"No, it is not really a tapestry at all, but a simple embroidery."

"Then what is so special about it?"

"It is one of the few hangings that has survived from Anglo-Saxon times. It dates to within ten or so years of the Norman Conquest. It was commissioned by William the Conqueror's half brother

148

Odo, who was the bishop of Bayeux. It tells the story of the Norman invasion and victory."

"That is what the names referred to! I remember there was a Willelm and a Harold—King Harold, of course. And an Eadward—who was he?"

"Edward the Confessor, the fellow who built Westminster Abbey. Harold was the brother of Edward's queen. Edward did not want Harold to become king when he died. There was a deal of skulduggery and an underhanded arrangement with William, but the upshot was that Harold was crowned king upon Edward's death. William felt he had some claim to the throne. He invaded England, defeated Harold at Hastings—you must at least recall the famous Battle of Hastings."

"Oh, indeed, on October 14, 1066. I studied it in history. Everyone has heard of the Battle of Hastings. That was the Norman Conquest—was it not?" she said uncertainly.

"Just so. Well, the Bayeux Tapestry is a depiction of those events on a strip of linen over two hundred feet long. The soldiers massing, the journey by ship, the arrival, the battle, and so on. The scenes include Harold's death from an arrow in the eye. Harold and his two brothers were killed, and on Christmas Day in 1066, William was crowned king of the English in Westminster Abbey. You may imagine how dear the tapestry is to the hearts of the French—their sole conquest of England. It is also of use to scholars as it portrays realistic scenes of life at that time—the sort of boats used, armor, and so on. Bonaparte made use of it to invigorate his forces earlier in the war by putting it on display in Paris. My muddle-headed thinking was that he would not use it again. That is why I took it."

He looked at her, expecting a blast of invective. Her eyes were aglow with admiration, and her lips trembled open in a smile of disbelief that made him feel ten feet tall.

"How splendid of you, Rotham!" she exclaimed. "And here I thought you were just a common thief, or perhaps a traitor. We must recover it."

He winced at her heedless words. "You do not think it foolish of me? I confess I was foxed when I did it."

"I should think one would require a little false courage for such an intrepid undertaking. I wish you will tell me all about it."

Rotham did not hesitate to re-create the daring of that evening in Bayeux when he had such a pretty and appreciative audience.

"Oh, I wish I had been there!" she exclaimed. "It beats anything, even a novel by Walter Scott. How Boney will stare when he goes to Bayeux Cathedral and finds it gone. Someone ought to write a ballad about it."

"I fear it will be hushed up—at least in England—if the Frenchies have recovered it. And, of course, if Louis is restored to the throne, no one will ever admit it was stolen. He might take it amiss."

"So your glory will go unsung," she said sadly. "What a pity. That is why you said you half hoped Boney did win, so that you would be a hero for having deprived him of the use of the tapestry."

"I was thinking only of myself. It was extremely selfish of me. Naturally I do not want—or expect—Bonaparte to win."

"We must recover it. It is vital." After a pause, she said, "Is that why you were urging the comtesse to go to Vienna, Rotham? Did you want her to return it en route?"

"Yes, I did originally think she might be helpful. She has, or claims to have, many friends in France through her connection with the Valdors. I had hoped something might be arranged, but decided it was too hazardous an enterprise for a lady. I never actually intended to join her there, if that is what you thought."

Miranda ignored his last speech and the implicit denial of any romantic entanglement with Louise. "Then she knows you have the tapestry," she said, with a meaningful look.

"I did not tell her so. I merely sounded her out on delivering an important message to France. The reason we were discussing it in my room was merely for privacy's sake. If I decided she would make a suitable agent, I would have showed it to her."

"You could have discussed it elsewhere, however," she said with a sharp look.

"I could, and should have done so. How was I to know you would come landing in on us? The important point is that someone discovered I had the tapestry. I wonder she did not take it when she had the opportunity."

"As you said 'she,' you are referring to the night Slack was drugged?" she asked.

"Yes, I have wondered about that. The silk skirt I felt in the Green Room—it might have been Louise, just trying to discover what was in the mysterious trunk. It seems the trunk excited some curiosity in the household. I wonder if she would even have recognized the tapestry and its significance. You did not."

"A real Frenchie would have recognized it, but Louise might not have. She would never have seen it, and she is not the bookish sort who might have chanced on that picture of it your papa and Berthier were looking at."

Rotham's lips quirked. "You did not miss much."

"I could never get a look at the book. Your papa took it upstairs. I should like to get a better look at the tapestry, now that I know its importance. One hears of a thing like the Bayeux Tapestry without having a clear notion what it really is, or looks like."

"When you spoke of a real Frenchie, you were referring to Laurent?"

"Or Madame Lafleur. And they are all three meeting in Brighton tomorrow. Perhaps you should go to Brighton."

"Perhaps I shall have to, but first we will speak to Macpherson."

On the outskirts of Hythe, Rotham stopped at a small whitewashed cottage on the sea. Macpherson's boat was out. It was used for fishing by day to lessen the suspicions of the Preventive men. Macpherson was at home, however. It was his son who fished by day. They found him at the water's edge, assessing the weather. Winds and tides and such things were of great interest to him in his profession. Macpherson was a stocky man with a red face and brindled hair.

"Ah, your lordship, you have come about your query," he said, walking forward to meet them. "I know nothing of the matter myself. I have had Meg, my good wife, drop a gentle hint among the homes of my lads. They none of them have heard a whisper about anyone sending a parcel to France. I will let you know at once if any of us are asked to do it."

"I would appreciate it."

"Mind you," Macpherson continued, tapping his nose, "it is possible the cargo will be shipped from farther along the coast. My territory runs from Folkestone to Rye. It would be up toward the South Foreland I am speaking of. Shall I put out the word?"

"If you would be so kind."

"With a handsome reward riding on it, you may be sure the territory will be covered. I will take a run east myself this very minute and let you know at once if I hear anything. If you do not hear from me, you will know no one has been asked to carry the parcel."

"Thank you, Macpherson," Rotham said. A golden coin passed invisibly from hand to hand during the course of a handshake.

"Good day to you, sir. And to the young lady. Miss Miranda Vale, ain't it?" he asked, with a sharp eye.

"Miss Miranda is spending a few days with Mama."

They left.

"It seems the tapestry is still in England, at least," Miranda said, to try to cheer Rotham.

"That still leaves a deal of ground to cover. We had best return."

They drove back to Ashmead.

Chapter Fourteen

Rotham's first concern upon reaching Ashmead was to go abovestairs to check on Berthier's progress. He was still pale as paper and unconscious. He had not spoken, but his condition had not deteriorated. In fact, the servant tending him had managed to get a few spoonfuls of beef broth into him.

Miranda felt she had been neglecting her hostess and went to the Tapestry Room to work on the perishing Flemish tapestry, while Lady Hersham continued her work at the high-warp loom.

"Hersham tells me you were in on certain exciting activities last night, Sissie," Lady Hersham said leadingly.

"Yes, Pavel awoke me when he found Berthier had been stabbed."

"Shocking for you! I do not know what your mama will think. Naturally we are very happy to have you, but if you would feel safer at home while all this horrible business is going forth, you must feel free to leave. Measles are not so serious as a murderer in the house."

"Oh, I could not leave now!" she exclaimed, with a thought to her evening plans with Rotham.

Lady Hersham studied her for a moment. "Just

how much do you know about all this business, Sissie?"

"I know about the Bayeux Tapestry," she said, feeling that said it all.

"Ah, so Rotham told you. It is a shabby thing. I was disappointed," she said, looking into the mirror image of her own work in progress. She had achieved a very fine effect with the shading of the trees. She was less happy with the depiction of Hersham and herself. They looked like a dumpy squire and his lady, and they had been an elegant pair, at least in their youth. In the Gainsborough portrait they looked much better. She was toying with the notion of adding gold threads to her riding habit.

As Lady Hersham had mentioned the tapestry, Miranda took it as carte blanche to discuss the matter. "Who do you think took it?" she asked.

"I will be blessed if I know."

"Do you think the comtesse or Laurent might be involved?"

"Not Louise Hartly. That was her name before she married her comte. She is not fool enough to jeopardize her reputation. She is petty-minded. She thinks only of Louise. It is shameless the way she dangles Laurent, waiting to see if he reclaims his family's estate. Then she would accept an offer fast enough."

"What of the comte?" Miranda asked.

"Laurent despises Bonaparte. One must not forget that he is a Frenchman, however. He might have been furious to think of the tapestry's being removed and plan to return it somehow. His reputation would be enhanced if he handed it over to Louis. It is very vexing. Very vexing indeed, but that is Rotham all over again. He never thinks of the family when he is indulging in these escapades."

Miranda felt a troublesome urge to defend Rotham. "He is very sorry, ma'am. I think he will be more careful in future. Do you not think it was a splendid gesture?"

A reluctant smile tugged at the mama's lips. It had less to do with admiration of the gesture than Sissie's defense of Rotham. Of all the ladies who had tossed their bonnets at her eldest son, Sissie Vale was the first one she actually liked. Perhaps it was because the girl had run tame at Ashmead forever, practically like a daughter. Some of the fine ladies she could tolerate, but she truly liked Sissie, and more importantly, it was clear as glass that Rotham was smitten with her. Such a welcome change from his usual flirts. He actually cared about her. Half a dozen times that morning he had sent a footman upstairs on some unnecessary errand, asking him to "just have a look to see what Miss Miranda is about" while he was up there. It was the Congress in Vienna, she thought, that had sickened him of the more worldly ladies.

There were no airs or graces about Sissie, and no simpering like her sister Trudie. She was a fine needlewoman and would be better when she had settled down. Naturally a young lady on the lookout for a husband could not be happy at the loom for hours upon end.

"Rotham is indiscriminate in his choice of gestures," she said. "This one would only be splendid if Bonaparte won and wanted to use the tapestry. I am of the opinion that he will not win, and England will find itself in the embarrassing position of having to explain why the thing was stolen. When Rotham chooses a wife, I trust she will be a lady who is not put off by his errant ways."

"He is not really so bad," Miranda said with a fond smile. "I expect Rotham will manage to smuggle it back into the cathedral. Returning it should be easier than stealing it, do you not think?"

"He is a clever enough rascal," the mama agreed. "Pass that red silk, dear. I am going to give myself scarlet lips, like a hussy. I have made my whole face too pink. The lips require red, or they will not stand out."

Miranda passed the red silk, and they continued chatting and working until it was time to change for dinner. Miranda wore the jonquil silk again. It was a quiet dinner, with no guests except Miranda, who was hardly considered company at all. After dinner the gentlemen remained behind to discuss the raid on Madame Lafleur's house that night.

"I can see it must be done," Hersham said reluctantly. "You see how these matters escalate, Rotham. What began as a boyish prank unsuitable to one of your years ends up with breaking into a private home like a common felon. I wish to God Berthier would recover, not only for his own sake—that goes without saying—but so that he might tell us who attacked him."

"Makepiece was here just before dinner," Rotham said. "He hopes for a recovery, but Berthier is too weak to question yet. Slack tells me Louise did not take madame's trunk to Brighton. I must discover if Lafleur has the tapestry. Surely you agree?"

"Yes, yes, it must be done. There is no trusting Lafleur. What do we know of her, when all is said and done? It was the comtesse who introduced her, and Louise would take up with anyone who speaks French. Are you taking Pavel with you?"

"Try and keep me away!" Pavel said. He reached for the port bottle with a dégagé air and knocked over his papa's glass.

"You have had quite enough, Pavel," Hersham said, and removed the bottle from him. Turning to Rotham, he continued, "For God's sake be careful. Lafleur may have someone guarding the thing, if she has it, which I sincerely doubt. With luck, it is on its way to France, and no one will ever know you took it. It is the best thing that could happen. We have only to deny we ever had it. They have no proof."

"What time shall we go?" Pavel asked Rotham.

"Around midnight," he replied.

That left a long evening to be got in somehow. It was spent in searching again those rooms already searched once, along with those rooms recently vacated by Laurent and Louise. It was not likely a tapestry over two hundred feet long and twenty inches wide was in the dustbin, but Pavel took a root through Laurent's dustbin anyway, just because it was there.

He lifted out a piece of crumpled paper and frowned over it. "Now this is demmed odd," he said. "It is a chit from the pawn shop in Rye. Laurent laid his diamond tie pin on the shelf."

"Poor Laurent," Miranda said. "He would want some cash for the holiday in Brighton."

"He certainly got it," Pavel said. "A hundred pounds."

Rotham reached for the chit and scanned it. "It is dated yesterday," he said. He knew his mama had given Louise a similar sum. Two hundred pounds was enough to get the tapestry to France.

Nothing else of interest was discovered. They returned belowstairs.

"Where shall I meet you, and at what hour?" Miranda asked Rotham as they went down the broad staircase.

"You ain't coming. This is men's work," Pavel said.

"Rotham said I could be lookout while you and he go inside to search. If I hear gunshots, I shall run for help."

"If you hear gunshots, it will be too late," Pavel said.

"Then I shall rouse the constable and catch them before they leave with the tapestry."

"What about us? Are you going to leave us to bleed to death?"

"Let me take a pistol, then, and I shall dart in and rescue you."

Rotham just smiled. "You would do it, wouldn't you?"

"I am an excellent shot. Pavel taught me with your dueling pistols."

He directed a quelling look at Pavel. "Did he indeed?"

"She could not hit the broad side of a barn door," Pavel said.

"I did so hit the barn door!"

"Yes, when you was aiming at the bluejay in a tree five yards away."

They joined the Hershams in the Blue Saloon. At eleven-thirty the older couple retired.

Hersham said in a low voice to Rotham on his way out, "Your mama does not know what you have planned. Come to my room and tell me what happened as soon as you return. I shall have a look in on Berthier before retiring. Good luck, son."

"Thank you, Papa."

Hersham gave Rotham's shoulder a paternal pat to show his trust, or love. With an image of Berthier stretched out on the bed above, he was seized with a fear that he would not see Rotham alive again. He could not understand this wild streak in his son, but he had come by it honestly. Hersham's younger brother Horatio was the same. Hersham could not comprehend, but he could love. He was not a demonstrative father. He just looked at his son, trying to convey thirty years' devotion in one look. Then he left.

Rotham had never seen just that sad look on his papa before. It made him feel a monster. What a wretched son he was. His voice was husky when he spoke. "Will you tell Boxer to have the mounts brought around, Pavel? I have concealed the pistols in a drawer here. Miranda, you should wear something dark."

Excitement glowed in her gray eyes. "Is it time to change?" He nodded. "I shan't be a moment," she said, and darted upstairs.

A soft smile curved Rotham's lips as he retrieved the pistols from the drawer of a bombé chest. Here was a lady after his own heart. His family, and indeed most of his friends, could not understand him. But Miranda Vale—she felt as he did. She did not rip up at him for one stolen kiss. She did not call him irresponsible for taking the tapestry. She realized that life was a game to be played to the fullest. With time he would grow sober like Papa. Having a son of his own, he felt, would settle him down. But

160

not yet. There was still this last rig to be run, and he was happy that Miranda was to be a part of it.

She was soon back. "I know I look perfectly horrid," she said, when he turned at the sound of her approach. "I found this old round bonnet and dark pelisse in one of the spare rooms today. I cannot risk destroying Trudie's good jonquil crape."

"Miss Vale, you look a perfect quiz," he said, but his smile softened the insult. She looked a perfectly adorable quiz. He wanted to take her in his arms on the spot and kiss her.

"I have already said so—and if you were a gentleman, you would disagree with me."

"Not if I were a truthful gentleman."

Pavel returned. "I told Boxer we were going out to show Sissie the badger sett. We had best hide the pistols."

Rotham handed him one of the lethal-looking weapons. They both concealed a pistol beneath their jackets and went out, with Boxer holding the door.

"Where, exactly, is the badger sett, Pavel?" Miranda asked in a loud voice for Boxer's benefit.

"Where it always is," Pavel replied. "In that spinney out back of the home garden. You must be quiet or you'll frighten them."

Rotham exchanged a wink with Boxer, who was not so blind or stupid as the youngsters imagined. He knew his lordship was running some rig. The main detail missing in his knowledge was the nature of the contents of the black trunk his lordship had brought back from Vienna.

"Any instructions during your absence, milord?" he asked.

"I do not expect any callers. If Lady Hersham

should, by any chance, inquire for Miss Miranda, you know where we are."

"Yes, sir. The badger sett. Just so. I shall wait up."

"That is not necessary, Boxer." They both knew this was mere chatter. Boxer would remain up and alert, until dawn if necessary.

The butler closed the door quietly behind them. With the house to himself, he went into the Blue Saloon and enjoyed a glass of Lord Hersham's excellent brandy. Just one. He knew how far he could go. Then he returned to his own room to await his lordship's return.

Rotham meant to help Miranda onto her mount, but she was too fast for him. She was in the saddle before he could reach her. He had looked forward to an excuse to have her in his arms. They headed down the graveled drive to the main road, three abreast, silent but for the clatter of hooves and the whisper of leaves. The tree-lined drive robbed them of seeing the night sky. It was not until they reached the main road that the moon came into view. It looked small and white and cold in the black heavens above, but it gave a good enough light.

There was no one else on the road, nor any ships visible on the sea beyond. The water rippled in the gentle breeze without forming white caps or waves.

On the outskirts of town, they tied their mounts beneath the spreading branches of a willow tree, out of sight, and proceeded on foot. When Rotham offered Miranda his arm, she put her hand gingerly on his elbow and smiled a shy, trusting smile. The town was virtually deserted by the time they reached it. Lights still gleamed in a few windows, but no one came to peek out and see their passing.

They moved swiftly, silently as shadows, along the High Street, turned off at Conduit Street, and went along to Madame Lafleur's small cottage. It was all in darkness.

"We'll try the back," Rotham whispered. They disappeared into the dark lane at the side of the house and found themselves in madame's vegetable garden. A detour to the left took them to the back door of a shed, a sort of lean-to attached to the house.

Rotham took Miranda's hand and led her aside. "You stay here. You should be safe behind that trellis," he whispered, scanning the yard for a place of concealment. He walked with her to the trellis at the side of the garden. Behind it, roses grew in profusion. Their colors were dulled to white in the darkness, but their perfume hung sweetly on the night air.

"If anyone comes, I shall hoot like an owl, three times," she whispered. "Perhaps you should leave the back door open, so you can hear me."

"Don't leave this trellis, whatever you do."

He gazed down at her pale face, washed in flickering shadows. Even in a round bonnet, she looked darling. On an impulse, he reached down and placed a light kiss on her cheek. She grasped his lapels and held on tightly.

"You will be careful, Rotham," she said in a small, frightened voice.

His fingers brushed her cheek. "Is it me you are concerned for, or the tapestry?"

"You. Both you and the tapestry. And, of course, Pavel," she added.

163

"I come first?" he asked.

She did not think this was just one of Rotham's flirtations. There was no teasing air about him tonight. He looked serious, almost tense with waiting for her answer. Yet with her knowledge of his character, she was too proud to tell him she cared for him. Perhaps he had looked like this when he kissed Trudie behind the lime tree.

"Just be careful." She scowled.

"I am seldom careful," he said, and with a reckless grin, he pulled her into his arms for a kiss that did not know the meaning of the word careful. It was a wildly passionate embrace that seared her lips and molded her body to his, there in the shadows. Her heart first fluttered, then wafted up to her throat, then slowed to a dull thud as the kiss deepened. She felt its throbbing pulse as his lips bruised hers and his arms crushed her ruthlessly, until she could scarcely breath.

What kind of fool was she? She had promised herself she would not fall in love with Rotham. But if this was not love, what was it? If anything happened to him, she would not want to go on living. She could not remember putting her arms around him, but when he lifted his head, she was clinging to him like a limpet.

"Oh!" she exclaimed softly. "Why did you do that?"

"Why do you think?" he asked in a husky voice. "Because I might never have a chance to do it again, and I could not die without kissing you, Miranda."

"You have kissed me before. Did you forget?"

"That did not count. It was before I loved you. I

do love you, my darling. Whatever happens—I love you."

Then he was gone, before she could tell him she loved him, too. She peered from behind the trellis as he worked at the back door for a ridiculously short time. Then he and Pavel disappeared, and she stood, watching, too overcome with joy and fear to think.

Chapter Fifteen

Once inside the shed, Rotham and Pavel stopped and listened a moment before proceeding further. All was silent. The back door into the kitchen proved harder to open. Pavel held his pistol at the ready while Rotham worked at it with a chisel. The lock gave with a light metallic click, and the door swung open. They knew that Madame Lafleur did not have any live-in servants. She had a couple who cooked and cleaned and tended the garden, but returned home at night. She might have some cohort guarding the house tonight if she did indeed have the tapestry, however, so they proceeded quietly into the kitchen.

It was tidy, except for a cup and saucer and teapot on the counter by the sink. Madame had obviously made herself a cup of tea before retiring. Rotham noticed there was only one cup, which was a good sign. He touched the pot; it was cold. Louise had mentioned madame would take the first morning coach, which left at nine. That being the case, she would likely have her trunk ready and waiting to be picked up. He would try the front hall.

He went cautiously to the doorway. It was a swing door with no catch. He pressed it lightly and saw in front of him a hallway. In such a small cottage, the kitchen was on the same floor as the drawing and dining rooms. He stepped quietly along the hallway, past the staircase leading above-stairs, and along toward the front of the house. The door to the street was visible; there was no trunk waiting beside it. Through the doorway on the left, he saw the outlines of a sofa, chairs, odd tables, and a grate. He tiptoed in and peered around. The trunk was not there either. It seemed it was still abovestairs, likely in madame's bedroom, where she could keep an eye on it.

He and Pavel would have to arrange some sort of mask, perhaps using their cravats to cover their noses and mouths, with their hats pulled low over their eyes when they went upstairs, in case ma-dame awoke and saw them.

Pavel tiptoed into the dining room. After a mo-ment he reappeared. "Psst! Found her!" he hissed quietly. "Hidden under the table. I thought it odd there was no chair on one side. Come along."

Rotham looked to the staircase. Finding no sign or sound of company, he went into the dining room. There, under the table, with a long tablecloth par-tially concealing it, sat a trunk. It pulled out qui-etly on the carpet. It was locked. Rotham did not want the bother of removing the trunk if it did not contain the tapestry. He applied his chisel again and lifted the lid. He knew as soon as he touched it that it was the tapestry. The cloth had the softness of bleached linen and age. He could feel the embroidery. He drew the trunk from the shadows closer to the window, to verify that it was indeed what he thought.

"What do we do?" Pavel asked. "Take the trunk, or just the tapestry?"

"We cannot carry a trunk on horseback. We just take the tapestry."

He scooped his hands under it and lifted it out. It was bulky, but by putting it on his shoulder he managed to carry it.

"Close the trunk; push it back under the table. If she comes down to check, she will suspect nothing until morning," he whispered.

Pavel did as he suggested, and they quietly retraced their route out the shed door. Miranda, watching from the shadows, saw them as soon as they came out the door. It looked as if Rotham was carrying an inert body over his shoulder. She ran forward.

"What have you done?" she demanded, aghast. "Surely you have not killed her!"

"Got the tapestry." Pavel grinned.

She looked to Rotham's face and saw Pavel's reckless, triumphant grin mirrored there. "I knew you could do it!" she said.

His heart swelled at her praise. "It will be a deuce of a job getting it home. We ought to have brought the gig."

"Or at least brought the mounts closer," she added. He must be feeling the weight of his burden. "Let us go and get the mounts, Pavel," she suggested. "Rotham cannot carry that all the way to the edge of town. You must hide until we return, Rotham."

"Not so close to madame's house. I shall move to the back of the garden."

"We shan't be long." She and Pavel left, running, to get the mounts.

"Went off like clockwork," Pavel crowed. "Could not have gone more smoothly if we had sat down

168

and planned it for a fortnight. I am the one who found it."

He entertained her with a recital of the adventure as they hastened to retrieve the mounts. They were soon back on Conduit Street. As the town was asleep, Rotham had decided to risk carrying the tapestry to the corner, to avoid the sound of horses going into madame's yard.

"We should have brought an extra mount at least," Miranda said, when they tried to arrange the tapestry in such a manner that it was safe, while still leaving room for a rider.

"I'll tie it to your saddle, Miranda," Rotham said. "You can ride with me."

"How can I? There is only room for one saddle."

"Hop up behind me and hold on tight."

That was the way they returned to Ashmead. Pavel rode ahead, holding the lead to Miranda's mount. Rotham and Miranda rode behind. She wrapped her two arms around his waist, happy for the excuse to be near him, holding him tightly, with her cheek resting against his back. Rotham held the reins with one hand. The other he placed over her hand, softly squeezing her fingers from time to time.

Miranda's mind was free to roam. "Whatever happens—I love you," he had said. And the very best had happened. They had recovered the troublesome tapestry without killing or hurting anyone else. Did he mean he wanted to marry her? Was it that kind of love, the kind she felt for him? She pictured a wedding, then raising their family. Her life would change, as Trudie's had changed when she married Parnham. There would be Seasons in London, meeting new people, then returning to winter at Ashmead. It all seemed like a dream. Perhaps it was only a dream. She wished they could ride like this, silently through the moonlit night, till morning.

They passed no one during the whole trip. Later, when he was gone, she remembered that hour as a magical time set apart from reality—her holding onto Rotham, him fondling her fingers. It seemed as if fate had arranged it especially for them, as a small foretaste of what life might have been, if only . . .

Too soon, they reached Ashmead. Pavel took the mounts around to the stable while she went with Rotham, who was carrying the tapestry, into the house. Boxer, wearing his coy smile, held the door for them. His eyes never strayed to the large object on Rotham's shoulder as he greeted them, so well was he trained.

"I trust Miss Miranda enjoyed seeing the badgers?" he said.

"They were lovely, Boxer," she replied, with a faraway look in her eyes.

"Will Lord Pavel be returning this evening, milord?" he asked Rotham.

"Presently. As you have waited up this long, you may as well stay another moment until he joins us."

"A glass of wine while you wait, milord? Champagne, perhaps?" he suggested archly.

"What an excellent butler you are, Boxer. Champagne, by all means. We shall toast the badgers. But first I must go abovestairs a moment."

He left, still carrying the tapestry over his shoulder. Miranda assumed he was reporting to his papa. He would check on Berthier as well, and hide the tapestry somewhere.

Pavel soon joined her, and behind him came Boxer carrying a tray with the champagne and glasses. Rotham remained abovestairs some ten minutes, discussing the matter with Hersham.

"So Madame Lafleur had it," Hersham said. He was in bed, wearing his nightcap. "Not in it alone, though, do you think?"

"I shouldn't think so. She was to join the Valdors in Brighton tomorrow. Either, or both, of them might have been involved."

"It could have been the modiste woman—she is a Frenchie. We know nothing of her."

"That is possible, but she is not going to Brighton, to the best of my knowledge. That is where the tapestry was headed, surely. It was Louise who suggested taking Madame Lafleur to Brighton to play propriety, yet I cannot see Louise wielding the knife that has put Berthier's life at peril. That suggests a man. How is Berthier, by the bye?"

"The same. Slack is to notify me if there is any change. Louise Hartly never was any good. I disliked having her under my roof, but she is your mama's cousin after all. She has a trivial turn of mind. I do not see her engineering the scheme, but she could play her part well enough."

"If Berthier recovers, he could tell us a great deal."

"Aye, and if he don't, we may never know. I wonder what they will do when madame shows up in Brighton empty-handed. Perhaps she will not go. It might be best not to pursue the matter. You have got the tapestry back."

"If it were only the tapestry, I would agree, but

there is Berthier to consider. One of them tried to kill him—perhaps succeeded. I am not of a mind to let the perpetrator off scot-free, Papa."

"Nor am I. There is nothing else to be done until morning, however. We shall have someone in Rye to see what madame does. Where will you put the tapestry tonight?"

"I plan to sleep with it."

"There will be a new bed companion for you," Hersham said with a scowling look.

When Rotham smiled, Hersham emitted a reluctant laugh. "Why could my first-born son not have taken after me, instead of Horatio?"

"I plan to improve, Papa."

"Aye, my brother was used to say the same. There is no going against nature. But you are a good lad when all is said and done, Arthur."

Papa had not called him Arthur since he had put on long trousers close to two decades ago. Rotham felt insensibly pleased. It seemed to acknowledge him as not only his papa's heir, but his son.

"I shall let you get some sleep now," he said, and left.

He stopped only to check on Berthier and have a word with Slack before returning belowstairs. He knew Slack would be waiting up to hear what happened.

"You got it back!" Slack exclaimed, when Rotham went to his room, still carrying the bulky bundle.

"As you see. I have to do a few things belowstairs. I shall leave it with you until I come up. How's Berthier? Has he spoken?"

"Not a word, but his breathing is a mite stronger, I think."

Rotham examined the pale face on the pillow. It

172

was nearly as white as the linen. No, he could not let the matter rest just because he had recovered the tapestry. Berthier was a colleague, fast becoming a friend. It was not over yet. Justice demanded that someone pay for this. But there was one victory to celebrate, and he was eager to go to Miranda.

He found her sitting with Pavel, patiently waiting until he came to drink the champagne.

"You should not have waited for me," he said, but he was pleased that they had.

"We want you to propose a toast," she said, smiling a secret smile that acknowledged their new relationship. Yet the smile was tinged with uncertainty.

Pavel poured three glasses of wine and passed them around. "Shall we drink to recovering the tapestry?" he suggested.

"To the tapestry—and to us," Rotham added, gazing at Miranda.

"To us," Pavel echoed, and they all drank.

The ensuing conversation covered the same subjects Rotham had discussed with his papa and ended the same way. They would wait until tomorrow.

"You looked in on Berthier?" Pavel asked. Rotham nodded. "How is he?"

"Breathing a little easier."

"Then I shan't disturb Slack when I go up. I am for the feather tick. We will have an early morning. The first stage leaves at nine, but madame may shab off on us earlier when she learns her trunk is empty. I shall be in Rye at seven. Will you come with me, Sissie?"

She yawned into her fist.

"Miranda needs her beauty sleep. Either Slack or I will go with you," Rotham replied.

Pavel had another glass of champagne and left.

"I wish it were all over," Rotham said.

Miranda shook her head. "You will only fall into some other scrape when it is, Rotham. A tiger does not change his spots."

"Stripes. Are you setting up in competition with Louise?" He set his glass and her own aside and took her hand. "This tiger has changed his stripes."

"Oh, but I like you the way you are—just a little dangerous."

"I will still be a tiger—just a tiger without quite such garish stripes. A more domestic breed of cat."

Miranda looked at him and shook her head. "I take leave to tell you, Rotham, there is not a domestic bone in your body."

He drew her to her feet. "How strange you should say so, when I feel a compelling need for domesticity."

Then he lowered his head and kissed her in a perfectly tigerish manner. When he held her in his arms, he knew his wilder days were over. He had been tamed by love. He had foolishly mocked his friends who underwent this transformation, never realizing why, or how, they could do it. He knew now they had no choice in the matter. It just happened. Papa would say it was growing up. If this was growing up, he had no objection, or regrets.

Chapter Sixteen

Miranda slept in until nine after her late night. The sky was overcast, which made her think, when she first awoke at her regular hours, that it was earlier. She was surprised to see Pavel and Rotham in the breakfast room when she went downstairs.

"Did you decide to send Slack to Rye to watch Madame Lafleur?" she asked Rotham, after they had exchanged greetings.

"We have been and are back, sleepyhead," Pavel told her.

She filled her plate at the sideboard and joined them. "What happened? Did she take the stage to Brighton?"

"Devil a bit of it," Pavel said.

Rotham was frowning. He said, "She reported the break-in to the constable. The story in town is that someone broke in and robbed madame of her clothes last night. I had a word with her myself. She came running up to me with eyes as big as saucers to lament her loss."

"Not a word about—anything else?" Miranda asked in perplexity.

"Not a word," Rotham said. "She is either innocent, which suggests one of the Valdors put the tapestry in her trunk, or—"

"Or a cunning rogue and a dashed fine actress," Pavel finished. "I would swear she had no notion what had really been in that trunk. Why would she make such a to-do of it if she was guilty? She would want to hush it up, would she not?"

"But it could not be the Valdors who put the tapestry in her trunk," Miranda said. "Laurent and Louise had already left. You recall madame's reason for going a day late was that she wanted Mademoiselle Chêne to finish her new gown so she could take it with her, presumably in her trunk. She would have seen the tapestry when she put the gown in."

"That points to Madame Lafleur," Rotham agreed, "although she might have agreed to carry the tapestry for them. But if so, why did she not dart off to Brighton or at least run off somewhere as soon as she knew she had been found out? Why raise a hue and cry about it?"

"Because it makes her look innocent?" Miranda suggested.

"And gives her another crack at the tapestry," Rotham added warily.

"Surely she would not be so brass-faced!" Pavel exclaimed.

"I am not so sure of that," Miranda said. "If she is the sole culprit, then she is bold enough to have knocked Rotham on the head when he found her lurking in the Green Room, to have stabbed Berthier, got the tapestry smuggled out a window, and returned to pick it up and take it to Rye. That suggests to me that she is brass-faced enough to try again. Where is the tapestry now, Rotham?"

"In my bedchamber, with the door locked and an armed footman watching it. Slack is inside the room with Berthier. Cook is personally preparing his meals and taking them to him to avoid tampering with the food or drink. If she gets at it again, she is not a woman, she is a witch."

"Well, it is all very strange," Miranda said. "How soon can you send the troublesome item back to Bayeux, Rotham?"

"I have had a dispatch from Castlereagh this morning. His orders are to hold on to it until we hear the outcome of things in France. He feels an armed confrontation with Bonaparte is imminent. If he wins, word will be leaked to France that England has the tapestry. If he loses, then the tapestry will be quietly returned with no fanfare."

"In other words, we are stuck with it for the nonce," Pavel said, not entirely unhappy with the chore.

"Just so," his brother agreed.

"Do you really think there will be another attempt to steal it?" Miranda asked.

"We have to prepare for the worst case," Rotham said.

It promised to be a long, troublesome day. Miranda was happy when Lady Hersham invited her to go to the village. The dame required a certain shade of blue for her *Ashmead* tapestry.

"For the stone walls will not all be done in gray, as you might think. There will be blue and purple in the shadows. If I can find just the right color—a sort of dusty indigo—I will be able to achieve the effect I want with one color, instead of having to blend them. It will make my work easier."

They got their bonnets and pelisses and went out to the crested carriage. Lord Hersham had confided the latest events to his wife.

"We shall call on Madame Lafleur while we are there and see if we can weasel anything out of her," she said as they drove along. "I do not usually call on her, but between her supposed chaperonage of Louise and her robbery last night, it will not look odd."

Miranda thought this an excellent idea. "There is no saying, we might catch her out somehow."

"She will not be so closely on her guard when it is only ladies calling," Lady Hersham said. "No one looks for any brains in ladies. Odd that it should be so, when it is men who have got the world into such a muddle, but so it is."

They purchased the threads for the tapestry first. Lady Hersham could not find exactly the shade she wanted, but decided to make do with a slightly brighter indigo than originally planned. The whole tapestry was much too bright anyway, from the pink face she had given herself to the scarlet lips. No matter. In a century or two, it would fade to a more delicate shade. Her work was destined for posterity.

Next, they called on Madame Lafleur. She was all smiles to receive such elevated guests. Her hair was slightly disheveled and her manner erratic. She answered her own door as she had dispensed with her servants for the duration of her visit to Brighton, which Lady Hersham learned was for the entire summer. She spoke of returning in September.

"And to add to the turmoil, the Crosses have found employment elsewhere," she lamented. "I am alone in the house, with my locks all—how you say?—broke. I have the locksmith coming around this afternoon to replace them. I have not even a *gâteau* to offer you, but I can give you the cup of tea at least. You *anglaises* always prefer the tea, *non?*"

She showed the ladies into her drawing room and disappeared for a moment to prepare the tea. She was soon back, flustered and flattered at the visit from the lady of the manor.

"You do not plan to go on to Brighton, then?" Lady Hersham asked, accepting a cup of tea and regretting the lack of *gâteau* to accompany it. "I am thinking of Louise and Laurent being unchaperoned," she added, lest the lady take the notion she was prying for some other reason.

"Tomorrow," she said. "I have written them the short letter explaining what happens. Your sons told you of my loss, I expect?"

"Indeed they did, Madame Lafleur. I am most sorry to hear it. The constable has not found the culprit?"

"Ah, *non*, but between us, I have no doubt it is the work of the Rafferty brothers. They were caught pawning Mr. Chester's silver in Hythe last year. What they are doing out on the streets so soon—*qui le sait?* Their cohort, Mr. Belton, claims they were at his house all the night playing at cards. The constable got a warrant to search their house, *mais bien entendu*, they had got my gowns out of the way before he arrives. Not only my gowns—my silver dresser set as well, a keepsake of my *chere maman*, along with a few bits and pieces of jewelry. My pearls." She shook her head sadly.

"I daresay it leaves you without a stitch to wear but the clothing on your back," Miranda said.

"*Heureusement*, I had not packed the new gown Mademoiselle Chêne was making for me. She was

179

to add the ribbons last night and have it ready by this morning, which she did, so, at least, I shall have it to wear in Brighton. Louise will borrow me a few gowns until I can get more made up."

"It is a shocking thing," Lady Hersham said supportively. "I shall have a word with Hersham. The fellows got right into your bedchamber, did they? You are fortunate they did not slit your throat while they were about it."

"No, my trunk was downstairs. Laurent, he helped Mr. Cross descend it yesterday when he and Louise stopped in on their way to Brighton. Laurent offered to take it with them at that time, but Louise felt it would be too much heavy for the horses. She had her own two trunks and, of course, Laurent's as well. They could have managed one more, but she was most eager to be off. You know how the comtesse goes. She was flying into one of her little pets. *Et enfin,* Laurent just helped Cross bring it down. It was too much heavy for Cross to carry alone. He—Laurent—arranged for it to be picked up this morning and taken to the stage at eight hours. I had it all strapped up and ready to go."

"But what of your new gown?" Miranda asked.

"Mademoiselle Chêne, she was to put it in a box for me and leave it at the coaching office to be put on the stage when I left."

"The thieves broke into your locked trunk then, did they?" Lady Hersham asked, sipping her tea and chatting as if she were just making conversation.

"Exactly. They might as well have taken the trunk. Of what use is a trunk without a lock?"

"Was anything else taken? The silver plate . . ." Lady Hersham inquired.

"*Non*, which is odd, that. What would the Rafferty brothers want with my gowns? They could sell them, of course, but they left behind items worth more than the gowns. The trunk was in the dining room, with a fine set of silver candlesticks sitting right on the table. Laurent had Cross push the trunk under the table so it would be out of the way. My cottage is *très petit*, as you can see." She looked around at the little drawing room.

Lady Hersham looked, too. She had never been in madame's cottage before. She was surprised to see such valuable bibelots and such good paintings hanging on the walls. If that portrait of an ugly female staring out a window was not a genuine Rembrandt, she would be much surprised. She knew for certain the Gainsborough was genuine. She had two of his works at Ashmead and recognized the brushwork. No one but Gainsborough had painted that bunch of trees, so lacy, with the sky showing between the leaves. He had put the exact same trees in his likeness of Aunt Sabina!

"I cannot imagine, me, how the fellows found the trunk," madame continued. "The cloth nearly covered it, and in the darkness, too." She shook her head in bewilderment.

Having discovered more than she had hoped, Lady Hersham quickly finished her tea and began to gather up her reticule and gloves.

"It is a great pity," she said. "It happens that Rotham brought back a few ells of silk from his trip to Vienna. I shall have him send you one. You can have it made up in Brighton. You will be leaving for Brighton tomorrow, I believe you said?"

"That is very kind of you, milady. I will be leaving on the first coach tomorrow, yes."

"I hope you enjoy Brighton. Give my regards to the comte and comtesse."

"Indeed I shall. Very kind of you to call, milady."

She saw them to the door, then closed it and breathed a sigh of relief. She had carried that off pretty well.

Lady Hersham was chirping merrily as they drove home. "Laurent is the culprit," she said. "I acquit Louise, after hearing she refused to take the trunk holding the tapestry. It was Laurent, you notice, who wanted to take it. When it had to be left behind, he hid it under the dining room table."

Rotham agreed when Miranda reported the news of the visit to him later. They met in the park, where she spotted him walking as the carriage arrived. When Lady Hersham slyly suggested she join him, to stretch her legs, Miranda did not hesitate a moment.

"Madame was lying her head off," he said. "The very fact that she was so eager to tell you all the details regarding the trunk is suspicious. It points the finger at Laurent."

"Your mama felt she had many valuable things in her drawing room. She mentioned some paintings. Madame claims to be poor. Do you think she is a thief?"

"I think she is involved, but she cannot be working alone. How could she have discovered the tapestry was at Ashmead? Only Laurent or Louise could have told her."

"Or Berthier, if he trusted her. He called on her the day he arrived."

"No, Berthier is a professional. He would not

reveal such a deep, dark secret. His call on madame had to do with obtaining brandy. She has connections with the Gentlemen. She supplies a few friends. I would like to be a fly on the wall when her letter announcing the missing tapestry reaches Brighton."

"Quite a comedown from a tiger," she joked.

He looked all around the park and, finding they were not observed, he drew her into his arms for a quick kiss.

There was only one other item of interest that afternoon. Pavel volunteered to take the ell of silk to Madame Lafleur, as he was eager to try his hand at pumping her for news. Upon his return he found Miranda and Rotham just as they were about to change for dinner.

"Madame's clothes were found," he announced. "They had been dumped into a ditch just east of Rye."

Rotham considered this for a moment. "Interesting, but not very helpful," he said. "Anyone could have dumped them."

"I think it is helpful," Pavel objected. "It lets madame off the hook. Why would she carry them to the edge of town to dump them when she could have burned them in her own grate? She had the whole night alone to do it."

"In this way, she gets her gowns back," Miranda mentioned.

"Yes, well, you have not heard the whole of it," Pavel said, with a quizzing grin. "The rat catcher saw someone dump the bundle, and it was not a lady."

Rotham's head jerked sharply. "When? When did he see this?"

"Early this morning, just before dawn. I had it of old Poldam, the constable. The rat catcher was on his way to Higgins's place to clear the rats out of the cellar. He saw a fellow carrying a bundle on his back, so, of course, he loitered about to see what it was after the fellow left. When he saw it was ladies' clothing, he put a couple of branches over the parcel to hide it and went on his way, planning to pick it up when he returned later. That was around four this afternoon. When he heard about madame's house being robbed, he knew he could not hawk the stuff and took it to Poldam."

"Were the silver brushes and pearls there?" Rotham asked, and waited tensely for the answer.

"There was nothing said about silver brushes or pearls. Just clothing. Poldam would have mentioned it if there had been pearls."

A small smile tugged at Rotham's lips. "Now *that* is interesting," he said. "Toward dawn, you say, this fellow was seen dropping his load?"

"About five o'clock this morning."

"Well done, Pavel."

Chapter Seventeen

Short of making sure the tapestry was secure, there seemed little that could be done unless and until the thieves made a second attempt. Rotham considered having a search warrant issued to search Madame Lafleur's house for the silver brushes and pearls, but he doubted such a cunning adversary would be unprepared for such a contingency. He was reluctant to let her know she was under suspicion. Thus far it was only a suspicion, after all.

Dinner was a subdued meal. The family could not discuss confidential matters in front of the servants. Lady Hersham's listeners displayed a greater than usual interest in her latest tapestry, while she explained the difficulty of its colors being brighter than she had planned.

"Indigo, eh?" Pavel said. "Not sure I should like to see Ashmead rendered in indigo. Er—what color is that, exactly, Mama?"

"A sort of violet-blue," she explained. "Comes from the indigo plant, I believe. It is more or less the shade of that new gown Selena was wearing when she visited last winter."

"Dash it, as I recall she was wearing a yaller gown," Pavel said.

"That was an afternoon dress, Pavel. At the large dinner party she wore an indigo gown. It washed her color out entirely."

"Why do you not use gray, like the stone of Ashmead?" he inquired, dragging the subject out to its limit.

"I did. It was the shading I was discussing, Pavel. The shadows created by the trees. If you do not use a different color, they do not show up."

"Your wits are gone begging, Mama. Shadows are black. Try black next time."

As she had begun her tedious explanation by the unsuitability of using black, she gave up. She had done her bit to enliven dinner. It was time someone else took a turn.

This subject exhausted, talk turned to the doings at Vienna and Bonaparte, but beneath the chatter there was an undercurrent of waiting and wondering.

After dinner the gentlemen remained behind for port and some more meaningful conversation. With no guests to be entertained, the ladies retired to the Tapestry Room. Lady Hersham decided it was time to begin instructing Miranda in the setting up of the loom. In her mind, it was as well as settled that she had found her successor.

When they heard the clatter of hooves outside the window, Miranda went to see who was arriving. She did not recognize the mount, nor did she immediately recognize Laurent, for she had never seen him mounted before. But as soon as she recognized him, she told Lady Hersham who it was and dashed off to the dining room to warn Rotham.

"Let me know what he wants," Lady Hersham called after her.

In the dining room, the gentlemen looked startled at this unusual intrusion of a female into their male preserve.

"Laurent is here!" she exclaimed. "He has just ridden around to the stable."

Three pairs of dark eyes, all strangely similar, stared at her. An air of tension grew in the silent room. Rotham was the first to react. He set down his glass, rose, and said to his father, "I shall meet him in the library."

"I shall go with you," Pavel said at once.

His papa put a hand on his wrist to detain him.

Rotham left with Miranda. "You will take a gun, Rotham," she said.

"He does not mean to kill anyone, or he would not have come so openly. He is just fishing for news. He's had time to receive madame's letter and get back to her."

"I would not trust him an inch. Remember what he did to Berthier." She had concluded that Laurent was the enemy.

He just squeezed her fingers, then left, looking somewhat strained. Miranda slipped into the Blue Saloon. She heard Boxer show Laurent in.

"May I have a word with you in private, Rotham?" he asked. His voice was calm, but it was not a natural calm. Miranda decided it was the calm of desperation. And desperation might easily lead to disaster.

"I have been expecting you, Laurent," Rotham replied. "Come to the library."

They walked down the corridor. As soon as the door closed, Hersham appeared in the hallway, with Pavel at his side. She ran to join them, happy to see that Pavel had availed himself of a pistol.

"Run along out of harm's way, Sissie," Lord Hersham said.

His forbidding aspect told her she could not remain in the hallway to listen, but she was determined to keep an eye on Rotham. Remembering that the court outside the French doors of the library gave a view of the room, she tore out of the house and around to the court. The curtains had been partially drawn to keep out the afternoon sun. She could see a portion of the room, high walls lined with books right up to the ceiling. Laurent and Rotham were already there. She could see them only from the waist up, for the long table impeded a complete view. They were having an earnest discussion, not angry, but grave. It continued for some time. Hands were thrown out in exhortation, heads moved violently. She had the sense that Rotham was asking questions and Laurent explaining.

At one point Rotham turned his back on Laurent and began to walk away. She wished he had not. What was Laurent doing? As she watched, he drew a pistol out of his waistband. Rotham stared at him in horror. She could see his lips open in protest, but she could not hear the words.

Rotham took a step back that put him beyond her view. Laurent followed, gesturing wildly with the gun, until he, too, disappeared behind the curtain. He was going to kill Rotham in cold blood. She ran forward and banged on the window to warn Rotham, or at least distract Laurent. Immediately there was a shot inside the room. Her blood turned to wax. She heard a wail pierce the silence, but did not realize it came from her own lips. She saw the hall door into the library open. Hersham and Pavel rushed in, stopped dead in their tracks, with horrified expressions on their faces. They rushed beyond view, presumably toward the scene of the carnage inside.

Her two hands were clawing at the window when Hersham heard her. He came to the window, gave an angry shake of his head, and drew the curtains closed. Her legs could no longer hold her. She sank onto the cold stone patio in a heap, not in a faint, but wishing she could faint, to ease the awful ache in her heart. She felt death would be preferable to the nightmare she must face.

She had no idea how long she sat there. The light lingered late in June. It was still twilight, but the shadows were lengthening. They did indeed cast a dark indigo shadow on the limestone walls of Ashmead. She remembered Lady Hersham had asked her to tell her what was happening. She must have heard the shot. She would be grieving, as Miranda was grieving. Yet it was a strangely objective sort of grief, because she could not bring herself to believe it. That would come when she had to look at his cold, lifeless body.

In her mind, there was no doubt that Laurent had killed Rotham. At such close range, how could he miss?

But perhaps he had failed? Perhaps Rotham, like Berthier, was not quite dead. She must go to him! She rose and entered by the front of the house, forgetting all about telling Lady Hersham. When she headed to the corridor leading to the library, Boxer stopped her.

"His lordship does not want anyone going there just now, Miss Sissie," Boxer said. She looked so young and vulnerable, with her dark eyes staring in a face as pale as snow, that the old childhood name slipped out.

"Is he—is he dead?" The words came out in a choked whisper.

"I fear so. His lordship did not call for the doctor. I believe they are taking the ... remains above-stairs."

Still the merciful objectivity remained. She felt she was playing a role in a drama; this wretched tragedy could not be happening to her. What must Miranda do, in this role? She must behave like a lady. She must think of others. "Does Lady Hersham—"

"She is with them. Run along into the saloon, Miss Miranda. I shall send you in a cup of tea."

Miranda just looked at him, then wandered off toward the Tapestry Room, not knowing where she was going. What did it matter? Rotham was not in the saloon, or the Tapestry Room, or anywhere. She was alone, and she half wished she had died with him. From the doorway she saw the four footmen go down the hallway, carrying a litter. Later—minutes or hours, she had lost track of time—they came out with the body. Hersham accompanied them, his head bent in grief.

She sat on her accustomed chair by the old Flemish tapestry. How strange that this lifeless piece of cloth could endure for centuries, while a vital force like Rotham could be cut down in a minute.

It was half an hour later when Pavel met Rotham in the library. Lord Hersham had sent Pavel off for the local magistrate to arrange matters with the utmost discretion.

"What happened?" Pavel asked. "You did not kill him, Rotham?"

"Of course not. I did not have a gun. He killed himself."

"Why?"

"Because Madame Lafleur betrayed him. When he received her letter announcing the tapestry was missing, he came rushing gallantly back from Brighton to take the whole blame for the imbroglio himself, only to discover she had already taken steps to put it in his dish. That was the last straw. Losing his estate was bad enough, being cast in the role of beggar when he was born to rule. He is not without pride. But for a Frenchman to be betrayed in love, on top of all the rest, was too much for him."

"You are not saying he loved Madame Lafleur? I made sure he loved Louise."

"So did Louise, but that was an act to divert suspicion from his real mistress, Madame Lafleur. As Louise was madame's friend, it made a convenient excuse for Laurent to call."

"Damme, she is too old for Laurent."

"It seems he prefers older women. Some men do. He let her coerce him into stealing the tapestry. The plan was to take it in triumph to Napoleon. She convinced him Napoleon would rise again, and his only hope of recovering his estate was to ingratiate himself with Bonaparte. When Laurent heard how she had tried to foist the whole blame onto him, he was undone."

"How did they find out you had the tapestry here?"

"Laurent was suspicious from the moment I brought that trunk into the house. He thought I had some secret documents from Wellington and wished to see them. He stole the key to my room from Papa's desk and managed to slip some laudanum into the milk for Slack's tea. He stopped Mary on her way to the room to ask if she had seen me. That was his excuse for being at the end of the corridor. He says he 'amused' her a moment. I expect we can translate that to mean he was flirting with her, which she would be afraid to tell us."

"I wonder why he did not steal the tapestry then, while he had the chance," Pavel said.

"It would have been better if he had. He recognized it, of course, but had no intention of stealing it. That notion came from madame, when he told her it was here. I believe she planned to take it herself, the night of the rout, when she knocked me on the head in the Green Room. That effort failed, however. As she did not have the liberty of the house, she needed either Louise or Laurent to help her. Not much question which she would choose— the other woman, or her lover, whom she could wind around her finger. She talked Laurent into it."

"What did he do with it after he stole it? It was not in the house. We searched high and low."

"It had already been slipped out a window, where madame was waiting to receive it. She had hired the gig at the stable in Rye that afternoon, claiming she wanted to call on Lady Valdor. Perhaps Laurent helped her load it. He knew what he was doing was wrong. I could see he had been troubled about something lately. He is not really wicked, just weak. He let her bearlead him, then when she was caught, she created a path leading to his door."

"All that talk about Laurent bringing down her

trunk, and wanting to take it to Brighton, and putting it under the table—was it all a sham?"

"That part was true enough. He did help Cross carry down the trunk. There was never any mention of anyone but Lafleur taking the tapestry to Brighton. She convinced Laurent that it was safer with her, she was less likely to be suspected and have her trunk searched. Of course, she wanted to keep it in her possession. She told him to his face tonight when he went running to her that she never intended to go to Brighton. Her destination was London, where she planned to sell it. She has French friends there, friends working for Napoleon's cause. I wondered where she got those valuable paintings Mama saw in her drawing room. She claims she cannot afford to set up a carriage. Laurent says they are from the Dupont estate in France, stolen at the time of the revolution. She has other French paintings as well, which Mama did not realize were valuable. Payment for past services to her French friends, no doubt. She keeps in close contact with the smuggling community and uses them for running messages to and from France."

"Who was the fellow who dumped her clothes in the ditch?"

"I have no doubt the 'fellow' was madame herself, wearing her late husband's trousers. I suspected as much when the rat catcher said the silver brushes and pearls were missing. She could not bring herself to throw them away. Her greed was her undoing—and Laurent's."

"Louise was not in on it at all?"

"He says not. He despises her, but by playing the role of suitor, she gets him invited here and other places. Her English connections were useful. That is the extent of the romance."

"I almost feel sorry for the poor bleater," Pavel said. "What we ought to do is send the constable after Lafleur."

"Too late for that. Laurent's Gallic passion overcame him. A *crime passionnel*, he called it."

"What does that mean?"

"It means, I fear, that he shot her when she threw in his face that she had been using him. I expect that is the main reason he shot himself, for he truly loved the baggage. He had not much to live for. His fate was gaol and eventually the gibbet. . . . All things considered, I believe I would have done the same. Let it be a lesson to us, Pavel."

"There is no trusting a woman."

"That was not my meaning. What began as a prank, my stealing the tapestry, has caused irreparable harm."

"Well, it has, but you cannot take credit for all the blame. I mean to say, if Lafleur wasn't a scoundrel, and Laurent a fool, none of this would have happened. Mind you, I do feel sorry for Berthier."

"Yes, indeed. Berthier, most of all. He was innocent, doing a dangerous job. If he does not recover—"

"Now, Rotham! You must not go shooting yourself. Damme, that won't do any good."

"I have no intention of shooting myself. You are looking at a reformed character, Pavel."

Pavel shook his head. "You don't look no different to me. I have heard that claim before."

"Now you will see it fulfilled. I must go to Miranda. She will want to hear what has happened."

"Try the Tapestry Room. She went in that direction when Papa would not let her into the library. I shall go along with you."

"I would prefer to go alone."

"Why? I thought you was reformed!"

"I am reformed, not dead," Rotham said, and left.

Chapter Eighteen

As darkness fell the image in the window grew clearer. When Miranda saw the reflection of a man rise up behind her, she stared in alarm, taking it for a ghostly image from beyond. It was Rotham! She stared harder at the window, checking the familiar lineaments. There was no mistaking the shape of his head, even with the uneven glass causing waves in it. He had come to take his final farewell. It seemed fitting, somehow, until she heard his voice speak.

"Miranda—what are you looking at?" Rotham asked, walking forward to join her at the window.

She did not turn; she was glued to the spot. Even her lips could not move. She had never thought a ghost would sound so natural. Then he touched her shoulder, and she leapt an inch from the floor. His two hands seized her shoulders, and he turned her to face him.

His heart plunged when he saw her expression. "You are disgusted with me," he said, gazing at her frozen mask of a face. "I cannot blame you. I am disgusted with myself. I never dreamed—"

Her lips hung open, quivering, as her eyes stared at him in disbelief. "Rotham?" The word came out in a muffled whisper, then the room grew dark with a bright orange light glowing in the center as she swooned in his arms. Real flesh and blood arms. She could feel his breath on her cheek, feel the substantial wall of muscle and bone against her chest. It might be only a dream, but she clung to him as if her life depended on it.

"I am sorry, my darling. I'm sorry," he said, his lips nuzzling her ear.

His head moved, and she looked up into his eyes. "Is it really you?" she asked, in a bewildered voice. "I thought you were dead, Rotham. I saw Laurent draw his pistol, heard the shot. They carried a body upstairs. Was it Laurent?" Rotham nodded.

"Oh, I am so glad! I mean—not happy he is dead, but— You shot him?"

The story had to be told again. They sat in the window embrasure, on the only seat in the room wide enough to hold two. Rotham held her tightly while he retold once more the painful tale of deceit and betrayal. He feared what she would say, or do, when it was finished.

She just looked at him with a wan smile. "I thought it was you who had been killed," she said, and buried her head against his chest, while a tremble shook her slender body.

"It would serve me well. I deserve no less."

She put a finger to his lip. "Don't say that. *I* do not deserve for you to be dead."

He pulled her fingers to his lips and kissed them, while uttering a silent prayer of gratitude.

"I do not deserve you, but I will, Miranda. You shall see. Marry me, and I promise you will not find a better husband anywhere."

She looked at him uncertainly. "Do you really mean it, Rotham? I would not like to go crowing at home that I have nabbed Rotham, only to learn that he has shabbed off the minute I left Ashmead."

"What a wretched opinion you have of me, and how well I have merited it. If this is a reference to Trudie, I want you to know I never offered for her, nor gave any indication I meant to."

"You kissed her."

"Indeed I did, but not like—this."

His arms tightened, and he kissed her with all the tender passion of a man truly in love for the first time. He felt no regrets for his tamer future, only for his crimson past. He wished he could have been better, for her sake.

The evening was busily spent arranging details of the sorry night's work. The constable had to be notified of Madame Lafleur's death. There was also the disposal of Laurent's remains to be considered. The vicar concluded he had been temporarily insane, which allowed interment in consecrated ground. There was no hope of covering the thing up entirely, with Madame Lafleur lying dead in Rye, but at least there would be no trial to incite public interest.

Lady Hersham decided tomorrow morning would be soon enough to notify the comtesse of the tragedy. She feared a Louise draped in crape mourning and shedding crocodile tears was more than she could endure. She would encourage her to return to Brighton in a week or so.

The affair was not even a nine day's wonder in the neighborhood. It was relegated to second place when word reached England the next morning that Bonaparte had been defeated at Waterloo. There was to be a grand celebration in Rye, with fireworks and a dance. Castlereagh immediately dispatched two of his most trusted aides to Ashmead to arrange a quiet return of the Bayeux Tapestry to France.

The Comtesse Valdor wrote a tearstained letter to Lady Hersham professing her most profound gratitude for all she was doing for *cher* Laurent. *Malheureusement*, she herself was suffering from a case of flu, and it was *tout à fait impossible* for her to come at this time. Did Lady Hersham think she need go into strict mourning for a brother-in-law that no one who mattered actually knew? Brighton was bursting with parties to honor Bonaparte's defeat. It seemed unpatriotic—indeed selfish—for the comtesse to go into mourning at this time of national rejoicing.

Lady Hersham could not have cared less if Louise took off her shoes and danced barefoot in the streets. She did not trouble herself to reply, for fear of being quoted as forbidding Louise to wear mourning. With luck, the hussy would find herself a new husband at one of the parties she wrote of. Hopefully an English one, so she could start speaking proper English again.

It was on the second day after learning of Wellington's victory at Waterloo that Berthier was well enough to speak. He verified that it was Laurent who had attacked him. He had heard surreptitious sounds in the hallway beyond the door and went to check, with his pistol drawn. Laurent had extinguished the lamps in the hall and lunged at him from the darkness with a knife before he had time to fire. By the light from his room, Berthier had caught a glimpse of Laurent.

"The tapestry?" he asked Rotham.

"It is on its way home. The war is over, Berthier. We won."

"We English," Berthier said, with a wan smile. "I believe it is time to anglicize my name to Bertram. And now I shall rest a little."

"I am sorry about all this, Berthier. I was a damned fool, and you paid the price."

"I am sure you will find a suitable reward for me. Some sinecure at Whitehall, or a knighthood, perhaps?"

"Consider it done."

The party to celebrate Rotham's engagement to Miss Miranda Vale was small and discreet. Only the two families were in attendance, including Lord and Lady Parnham, who made the trip of twenty-five miles for the express purpose of trying to talk Miranda out of such a misalliance. They might as well have saved their horses the trip. Miranda only laughed at their dire warnings.

Rotham had changed. Like any new convert, he was quite fanatical about his reformation, but she knew that would not last, nor did she want it to. For Rotham to be sensible and dull would be like a unicorn losing his horn and becoming just another horse. She preferred the romance and excitement of the unicorn. She had fallen in love with the old Rotham and meant to resuscitate him. There were rumors of Napoleon trying to escape from France by boat. Some even said he would seek safety in England. Rotham had a fine yacht.

"Let us go on a cruise for our honeymoon," she suggested.

"We shall tour the Greek islands."

"Oh, do you think all the way to Greece? I thought perhaps France. . . ."

Rotham met the challenge in her twinkling eyes. "The *on dit* is that he will head for Plymouth. A nice tour of Lyme Bay should put us in the vicinity."

"I should love a honeymoon at Lyme Bay of all things!"

"And in the worst case, if Boney does not come to England—you know I always like to prepare for the worst case—we still have the more customary delights of a honeymoon. I half hope he does not interrupt us."

"Meeow! Your stripes are fading, Rotham!" she scolded.

"You know how to bring out the beast in me," he said, but as he attacked her, he did not seem to need any help.

A lovesick young man, a fiercely protective older sister, and a bemused man of status and power add up to adventure and romance in **JOAN SMITH'S**

KISSING COUSINS

Samantha's younger brother is accused of theft, but she knows it is the flashy older woman he's been seeing who is to blame. Samantha turns to her stuffy but influential cousin Salverton to help. Salverton thinks his cousins are nothing but trouble...until the headstrong Samantha begins to steal his heart. That's when the real fireworks begin.

Coming to your local bookstore in December 1995.

Published by Fawcett Books.

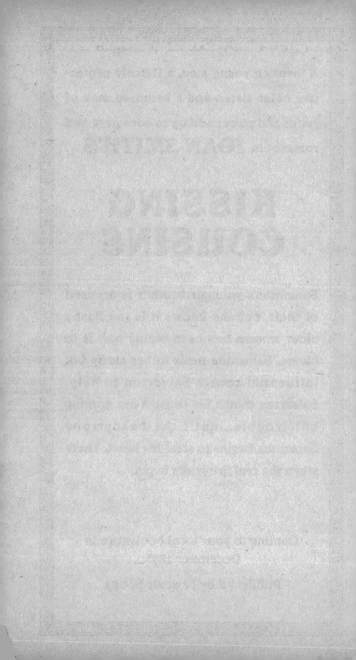